I0673585

SCAN THE QR CODE BELOW

for reviews and to purchase your copy today!

Copyright © 2024 All rights reserved.

No part of this publication may be reproduced,
stored in a retrieval system, or transmitted in any
form or by any means, electronic, mechanical,
photocopying, recording, or otherwise, without
the prior written permission of the author, except
for brief quotations used in reviews or scholarly
works.

Printed in the United States of America

Second Edition

Published By Beth M Winters

bethmwinters@gmail.com

This is a work of fiction. Any resemblance to
actual persons, living or dead, events, or locales is
entirely coincidental.

Table of Contents

Chapter 1 Indiana, 1924.............................1

Chapter 2 The Madisons.......................19

Chapter 3 The Mastermind 33

Chapter 4 Doctor Stone 53

Chapter 5 a party instead of a picnic 73

Chapter 6 Tea Roses and Tears 90

Chapter 7 Cholera................................110

Chapter 8 Becky's a Peach 123

Chapter 9 A river like a sunken mirror.............139

Chapter 10 A perfect rattle-snake!......................164

Chapter 11 The Spanking 183

Chapter 12 All Clad in White 198

Chapter 13 Mountain Country, Utah 214

Chapter 14 Will You Sing For Me 228

About The Author................................237

WILL YOU SING FOR ME

A Historical Mormon Romance

by

M.E. KNICKERBOCKER

Chapter 1 Indiana, 1924

The sun was beating down unmercifully upon the dusty country road that wound gently in and out among the giant sycamores along side the peaceful, majestic Wabash River. It was late August of 1924. Jane and Charlotte Pendelton, with their mother, Cora, and Aunt Em Ulrick, were returning from church in their new car. They were going at a lively speed along the river road when Jane passed another car before Aunt Em could see who was in it.

"Mercy on us, Jane Pendelton, don't drive so fast! Who could that have been - we just passed?"

"That, Auntie dear," replied Jane, "was the Madisons."

"Of all things! Looks to me like their car is just about another one-horse shay," commented Cora, her heavy features flushed quite red.

Jane drove swiftly and with steady hands. Having come this far over rather hilly country, they now reached a rather low place in the road. The sycamore trees spread their enormous boughs over the winding road, and through their open spaces the sunlight flickered on the smoothly flowing river. This was the section of the river road which ran directly in front of the Madison homestead. It was also an ideal place for lovers to linger, and here they often came in the cool of the evening, some to sit and talk together, others to take a canoe and dream while they drifted.

"For pity's sake!" gasped Charlotte. "I never noticed the place when we went by this morning. What on earth have they done to it?" She stared at the old mansion-house.

"I think it's high time myself," answered her sister sarcastically. "To think people will let Virginia creepers cover the entire ends of the house, chimneys and all, is beyond me. But it's just like the inmates of that house to do such things. Rather hair-brained, really, like somebody who needed a haircut."

Jane's tones were icy. Anyone could tell she was about as much kin to the Madisons, spiritually, as a saber-tooth tiger is to a domestic cat.

It's just too bad. Now it isn't half as picturesque," moaned Charlotte, ignoring her sister's irony.

"If that's the quality you are hankerin' after, honey," said Jane, "there's plenty left. Look at all those honeysuckles and climbing roses rambling in perfect confusion over the porch-pillars and around those old twelve paned windows. For my part, I like something more practical, I'd yank 'em all down and give the place a good stiff coat of paint. I'll bet my last nickel the weather-boarding is all rotted!"

"I don't see how you'd do that, Jane." Cora's tone was absolute. "Paint is expensive. That place has a mortgage plastered on it worse than old Uncle John Gilmore's, and it takes everything they can rake and scrape to meet it."

It made no difference to Cora Pendelton that her own place was under a second mortgage. Being a woman of the common field-daisy variety, she was prone to see saw-logs in other people's eyes, when her own eyes were so full her vision was obscured.

I'd fix that mortgage in a hurry if 'twas me," said Aunt Em with a wave of her plump hands. "What did the Lord plant all them black walnut trees fer, right there in that front yard of their'n? I'd sell 'em and save my gray hair!"

"My gracious, that would be awful, Auntie. I just dote on walnut trees," said Charlotte. "If they ever do that, I'll cry my eyes out. There isn't a handsomer grove in all Indiana."

"I wouldn't cry over a little thing like that," said her mother. "Their lawn is too big for any use and the sycamores along the river are trees enough. But

3

personally I always have thought Lucy Madison was a little bit queer."

Cora's downward-bowed mouth had suddenly grown very straight and prim. She said nothing more but remembered how she had asked Lucy Madison that very morning if she and her family didn't want to join the new secret society. Somehow the impression had been definitely left upon Cora's mind that Lucy did not exactly approve of such things.

"She isn't the only one that's queer," tersely remarked Jane over her shoulder as she drove faster than ever. "You should have heard the remarks Becky made in class this morning."

"What did she say?" demanded Cora, sitting up straight.

"Well, Mrs. Thatcher asked the class why miracles were no longer performed in our day," replied Jane. "Some of them said it was lack of faith like the ancient apostles had. But Becky—well, it stumps me yet—she said that had nothing to do with it. People were just as firm in the faith as ever, but the real secret of it was that we had no one among us with the right authority to really administer in the name of the Lord."

"Land sakes," sighed Charlotte, "I thought Sara Thatcher never would quit looking at her so straight."

"Well," said Cora in a reserved, hard tone, "she needed it! The idea of a nineteen year-old slip of a girl like her making such a remark, and with Reverend Emery visiting that class today. He's one of the best ministers we've ever had here. It's those confounded books Lucy lets her read, mark my word!"

"That was a reply that woke everybody up, and a real one, to my notice," said Charlotte. "How do you know she isn't right about it, Mother? History is so vague to most of us concerning the time between the end of the ancient church and the beginning of . . . ."

"Of all things, Charlotte Pendelton!" interrupted Cora, gasping outright.

"Well anyhow, Mother, I'm glad she said it. It gave me a thrill. I get so tired of going to Sunday School and hearing no new ideas."

"Don't say that, Charlotte," sighed Aunt Em wearily. "All decent folks go to church even if it is kinda stale. We jes' don't talk much about it, that's all."

"If I had my way," retorted Charlotte a little warmly, "we'd quickly jerk Sara Thatcher out of teaching that class. Becky knows more about the Bible than Mrs. Thatcher any day."

"Maybe she does know more about the scriptures, I don't know," replied Cora skeptically, "but it's mortal certain she don't hold the social position in the neighborhood that Sara Thatcher does."

"No, I know she doesn't," Charlotte admitted dejectedly, "but Sara Thatcher's mind is rusty. Becky's is as bright and new as a brand-new silver spoon on a wedding table."

"Becky Madison has a fine mind." added Aunt Em dryly. "She gets that from her Ma's side of the family, but it's a downright pity her opinions are as they are."

"Yes, sirree!" added Cora emphatically. "Such opinions can easily prove to be the ruination of anyone."

"I don't know of anyone anywhere," flamed Charlotte, thinking of how much she loved Becky, "with more fixed opinions than Sara Thatcher. If she can't have her way about things in the church, she proceeds to break it up. I think she lacks the Holy Spirit and is up there just to show off. She does not like Becky to come into her class because it puts her in such a bad light."

Charlotte paused, breathless and bewildered, scared and surprised at herself, to think she had dared say so much in defense of her friend. She could sense the unfriendly attitude of her family toward her now that she had spoken out in Becky's defense, but with a flash of her keen gray eyes, she maintained her stand.

"It's plain to be seen," whispered Aunt Em to Cora behind her open fan, "Charlotte is seeing too much of the Madisons."

"You're right there, Em. I see it now. Leave it to me. Becky does nothing but read, and when she isn't doing that, she's playing that wild music of hers on the piano!"

"They call it 'gypsy music', Cora," mocked Em.

"I don't know what they call it," emphasized Cora intolerantly, "but such stuff ain't civilized to me!"

"Well, anyhow, I think her music is lovely!" replied Charlotte a little stubbornly. "In fact, everything Becky does is wonderful, which is exactly why that restful old house is such a beautiful setting for the Madison family."

"Of course, it is, darling," crushingly cut in Jane. "Being Early American in style and full of antique junk, it wouldn't go with anyone else."

The blood in Charlotte's veins surged up quickly under her sister's sarcasm but she gaily replied, giving 'tit-for-tat' with gracious smiles. "Of course, precious, the place

7

will no doubt someday be turned into a museum, and your intrepid offspring, going there for instruction, will adorn its spacious rooms."

Jane gave Charlotte a withering look but said no more. It was a well-known fact in the Pendelton family that Charlotte dearly loved children and was patient with them, but Jane, being of a self-centered disposition, openly disliked them, calling them "brats." It always made her furious when she was teased about her future children that she vowed she would never have.

"The reason you stand up for Becky and that place," Jane sneered, biting her lips, "is because you like Andy, her brother!"

Charlotte openly giggled. "Oh Jane, how well you read my mind. But that is not saying what he thinks about me."

"There now, Corie, what did I tell ye?" whispered Em with a wink.

"There's not going to be a Madison in the Pendelton family if I can help it. No siree, Em, no writers! No painters! No musicians for me. I like practical folks who bring in the dollar!"

"That's what counts in the long run, Violin music, Corie, is a terrible ordeal to me, and Andy Madison is worse than usual."

Jane quickly turned the car here, into their own lane, and soon stopped beside a very modern blue-brick bungalow which sat on a little hill. There was not a single tree to keep it company, save a few half-grown fruit trees in the backyard.

With flushed cheeks, Charlotte sprang from the car and walked briskly to the house in front of Jane. The older women, still talking, were left to come in at their leisure.

Upstairs, Charlotte smiled broadly over her little tiff with Jane as she changed her silk frock for a neat house dress. It wasn't often she could hold her own with Jane, but she was learning.

When she appeared in the spotlessly clean kitchen, which she had worked so hard the day before to put in shining order, her mother was completing the filling for a lemon pie. Cora poured the filling into the delicately browned pie shell and piled the meringue on top, spreading it out in little heaps here and there.

She was just going to set the creation in the oven to brown when a small boy, lean and badly freckled, opened the side screen door.

"What's that, Ma?" He said, winding a bunch of string around his hand.

"Go 'long," frowned Cora. "Don't you see I'm busy?"

"Gee, that's sure some soap-suds on top, Ma. Where'd ya learn – that's fatter than you've been making? Did Sis here teach ya?"

"No, she didn't," snapped Cora, exasperated. For that matter she was always out of patience with this small son. He had such an uncanny knack of tracing things to their proper origins.

"Get out of here, Leander, I'm not foolin' with you now!" Cora pushed him roughly aside and turned him toward the outside door.

"For pity's sakes," she began again. "What's that you got dangling on a string out of that hole in the back of those overalls I just got done patchin'?"

Leander screwed his wiry little body halfway around at the waist and glanced with a grimace over his shoulder.

"Little peas and button hooks!" he exclaimed, surprised, rubbing the well-padded part of his anatomy with a dirty, freckled hand. "I had it in my pocket—musta crawled through my overalls from my pant's pocket when I tore that hole on Madison's back pasture fence."

"You been in that swamp again?" demanded Cora. "Didn't I tell you to stay out of there huntin' queer things?"

"Aw Ma, but ain't it a cute little bugger?" pleaded Leander.

"Cute nothin', get out of here with that thing. You give me the creeps!" Cora was aghast to see Leander, with twinkling eyes, draw a small yellow and green lizard up on the string until it rested in the palm of his grimy hand.

Now thoroughly upset, Cora made a dive for the broom handle. Leander, well aware of what was coming, escaped into the backyard.

"You're just like your Pa," she exploded! "I never can catch you in anything, and I never know what you'll do next!"

"Save me a piece of pie, Sis," Leander called from the backyard. Charlotte did not answer but mentally decided that she certainly would.

"Set the table, Charlotte, we're late already." Cora's manner became less irritated but still the waters were not placid.

"I think, young lady," she began, changing the subject but not her tone, "the best thing you can do is not to take up with the Madison's notions too strongly and let young men of that family slide. They are not welcome here!"

If Cora expected Charlotte to say something to that, She was disappointed. Charlotte maintained a stoical silence, but her cheeks gradually became more and more pink until they were quite flushed. Her father at the dinner table wanted to know if she had a fever but Charlotte shook her head and remained silent. Tom Pendelton drew his own conclusion; Cora had undoubtedly been up to something again.

After dinner, everyone went about their own desires, so Charlotte took a new book on interior decoration and wandered away to the quiet woods at the back of the farm. There, sitting on a fallen log in the thick shade of the beech trees, she began to ponder over the day's events, coming to the conclusion that jealousy was at the bottom of the criticism of Becky and her family.

"Why, there is not one in our family that can hold a candle to Becky, and both Mother and Aunt Em know it." she mused while examining a fern frond. "Ever since Mother saw Cecil Manning at Becky's party, with Jane as a dinner partner, she has never rested, putting on airs. I don't blame Becky for not liking Cecil. All he thinks about is money and going to some show place. There is no depth to him, it's just a matter of fascination with him, which he will quickly get over."

"As for Mother telling me to push Andy away. I have a right to choose my own way, just like she did! Becky and Andy are both clean mentally and inspiring to know. I wish I could get out of this rut I'm in. Life seems to have a lid on it, and I'm forever bumping my head against it."

Thereupon Charlotte ceased to think anymore about the problem but fell to contemplating the beauty of the wild trees and plants around her. She soon became lost in the intricacy of the wonderful color harmonies and designs of nature's leaves. Every design is so quiet in color scheme, the tones blending like a theme of music. It inspired her and made her realize that there undoubtedly was a Glorious Being who had created it all and who forever was the Supreme Ruler of His works.

Gradually peace came back into Charlotte's mind, bringing faith, hope and tolerance in all things, hence to her the world was once more a fitting place in which to live. As she sat there, she forgot her book. The song of a cardinal deep in the woods thrilled her—her heart burned at the sound of its call. Surely it had a mate somewhere in the pawpaw thicket. Charlotte watched to see the cardinal, but failing to see it she arose from the log to go home.

"Don't go yet," exclaimed a familiar voice somewhere out in the spicewood beyond her.

Her eyes, following the track of sound, saw Andy sitting beneath a twisted ironwood on a lichen-covered granite boulder.

"Andy Madison!" she exclaimed, her eyes brightening, "how long have you been over there?"

"Long enough to know this bit of woods," he replied gaily, "as much by heart as you do."

"Do you really like the woods as much as I do, Andy?"

"I don't know about that, but I never tire of it," and he crossed the open space between them and sat down on the log beside her.

"I never tire of it either. It soothes me when I'm tired and I find it more interesting than lots of people."

"Am I included in the 'lots'?" queried Andy gently.

14

"I never hinted at such a thing, did I?" protested Charlotte.

"Thank goodness," breathed Andy with a look so warm and tender in his eyes that Charlotte's heart missed forty beats and she could not look into his eyes any longer.

"Charlotte, can't you look at me like that again? It warms my heart! Why do you always look away, dear? It was meant to be that we should love each other."

Andy's voice was something Charlotte always loved to hear. It had such a manly quality to it—so soft and rich. As her heart stood still, he took her hands, and she felt this was something so joyous she could hardly bear it. It caused the wings of her soul to flutter in a wondrously sweet holy song.

"Why do you love me?" she asked simply, looking deep into his eyes.

"Because God told me to. You are mine, darling, and I am yours and it will always be so."

Like the hush of hummingbirds gliding gently upward to the nest upon the bough, Andy took Charlotte to his heart.

There was something so sacred about this tender statement that it touched her beyond power to express. There was a quality about it so certain, it became law. Freely and joyously she pledged herself to become his wife, for she knew that she loved Andy Madison and that it was between them just as he had said.

Then it was as it has been with all true lovers since Time began—a million things to whisper and the answer to read in each other's eyes. She listened rapturously to everything until he began to tell her about his faith and expressed the hope that they could be married in the "Temple of the Lord."

"For," said he, "darling, we loved before we came here, in the Spirit World, when we had our youth in our Father's glorious home. Now that we are here, dear, I want to seal you to me forever, that we may never part and you'll be mine through all Time to come. You see, Charlotte, there is no giving in marriage in the next world. We must do all that here."

"I don't understand, Andy. Doesn't your marriage service read like ours?"

"No, sweet, it does not. When we marry in the Temple we are married for Eternity as well as for Time. We promise to keep all the commandments and you become my Queen and Priestess forever. We become heirs to the Celestial Kingdom to arise in the First Resurrection and take our places beyond all the holy angels to reign as lesser gods before Him who is Lord of all and King of Kings."

"I don't understand it all," breathed Charlotte from the shelter of his arm. "I am afraid, Andy Madison, it is entirely too breathtaking for me to conceive of it. My brain will have to become educated to it."

Thrilled beyond words at the way Charlotte had taken his last hope, Andy promised to bring her some literature that would help her to understand.

"Then you can study it over and see if my views are not reasonable and correct," he said.

"That does make love such a noble thing," she sighed gently.

"Of course it does, and so it is. True love does not end at the grave but goes on forever and ever, as our Heavenly Father intended it should."

Because it was late they soon parted, with Andy promising to put the literature that evening under the leaves of a giant burdock close by where they sat. Each realized the day had been an important one in their lives and henceforth the old life was gone forever. Come what may, they agreed to join their respective paths of life together until one or the other slipped through the Silent Door.

Chapter 2 The Madisons

"Good morning, Grandpa," Becky cried joyously "How are you today?"

"Foine, dearie—faith and ye air up early! Me' thinks yer eyes now can't be any bluer than the sky, and those red lips—what was it they be singin' just now?"

"Oh how lovely was the morning
Radiant beamed the sun above.
Bees were humming, sweet bird singing, Music ringing through the grove.
When within the shady woodland,
Joseph sought the God of Love.
When within the shady woodland,
Joseph sought the God of Love.

"Humbly kneeling, sweet appealing T'was the boy's first uttered prayer
When the powers of sin assailing
Filled his soul with deep despair.
But undaunted still, he trusted
In his Heavenly Father's care;
But undaunted still, he trusted
In his Heavenly Father's care."

Becky's voice rose clear and sweet, full of faith and with that same power which comforted the youthful prophet.

"B'gorra, tis a pity ye air a wastin' a foine voice like that on an old critter the likes o' me," exclaimed Grandpa Mahoney with misted eyes. "Shure an if Oi found meself the possessor of a voice so sweet as all that in the next world, Oi'd niver be after makin ould Gabriel any trouble, Oi'm think-in', cause he niver set me down in a foiner place."

"Aw, Grandpa, you know I always try to sing my best for you. I don't know what I'd do without you to praise me once in a while. Wasn't that a great day," explained Becky, clasping her hands, "when Joseph went into the woods to pray?"

"Faith now, but 'tis the best of truth ye do be spakin', colleen. B'gorra but the thought comes often and Oi almost take l'ave o' my sense thinkin' how this grove here, bein' so peaceful like, might somehow be like that other grove. Shure many a time it is Oi've had a foine time deludin' meself."

"It is just about like it, to my mind, too, Grandpa. Do you want me to sing the last verses too?"

"Suddenly a light descended
Brighter far than noon day sun,
And a shining glorious pillar
O'er him fell, around him shone.

While appeared two heavenly beings
Got the Father and the Son,
While appeared two heavenly beings
God the Father and the Sun."

"Joseph, this is my Beloved,
Hear Him, Oh how sweet the word!
Joseph's humble prayer was answered
And he listened to the Lord;
Oh what rapture filled his bosom,
For he saw the living God.
Oh what rapture filled his bosom,
For he saw the living God."

"Oh," breathed Becky in a hushed way, "I would have loved to have seen what he did, Grandpa!"

"Oi am afraid Oi'd niver lived thru it. We can be glad we heared the blessed news and believed it. For my part Oi'm allus rejoicin' over it. It shows, Becky Colleen, that the Almighty is still the same yesterday, todey, and termorrow."

"I love it too, Grandpa, with all my heart."

"Promise me, Becky, that ye won't be forgettin' Grandpa's temple work. If it wasn't fer this auld heart agoin' back on me—Oi would tend to me duties meself."

Becky drew near and took his feeble hands. "There now, Grandpa, don't you be wearying yourself one bit about all that. Andy will be ever thinking of you and the work will be done—so don't be fretting any more about it."

With a loving pat here and a deft little shove there, Becky soon had her grandfather propped up in bed so he could look from the upstairs front window out across the lawn, through a hundred intervening branches of staunch old walnut and on through the mottled sycamores to the shining river's brim.

While Becky put the other upstairs rooms in order, Grandpa Mahoney sang gently under his breath. Sometimes she heard the verses of that grand old hymn Grandfather had learned as a sectarian, "Blessed Assurance," but more often it was the deeply soul-satisfying lines of "I'm the Child of a King," Then it came to those glorious lines--.

"An exile from home, yet still I may sing
All glory to God, I'm the child of a King."

Becky in the adjoining front room, in silent wonderment, shook her head and meditated upon the enormous spiritual growth and power of her grandfather. A fervent prayer unconsciously ascended that she might be blessed in the same manner.

Who could say this aged man was not happy? White, worn and extremely thin with suffering, he stood within the "shadow of the veil;" but, though broken like a mighty oak of the primeval forest when smitten by heavy lightning, his spirit refused to bow to the depths of despair.

He was content with the little things of life, neither did he care any longer whether he was happy or not. In every way possible he sought to bring comfort into the lives of those about him. If he had a moment of sorrow, he drowned it in a song. If he shed a tear because the pleasures and beauties of youth were no longer his, he anticipated the glories of Eternity, where age never comes and the intelligence is always progressing in beauty and power. The result of all this philosophy was, he lived a life of inspiration to those about him, and was supremely happy. With a sincerely humble spirit, he tried to live the Law as he understood it, trusting in his Heavenly Father for every breath he drew—and was constantly upheld by the power of the Holy Spirit, that wonderful, most gracious healing power, which cast all shadows away and gave peace beyond understanding. So he looked, with a song on his lips and joy in his heart, out through the branches to the sky above. To him each twig bore an emerald; the little open spaces of fathomless blue were sapphires.

To Becky's satisfaction, his eyes soon closed. She softly drew the shades behind the white ruffled curtains and slowly closed the door of the dear old-fashioned bedroom that had long ago become a shrine. She descended the stairs and went to the kitchen, where she found Mrs. Hudnut, an old neighbor, talking to her mother.

"Hello, Becky dear," greeted the old lady.

"How are you today, Aunt Elvira?" said Becky, returning the greeting graciously.

"Fine—fine, it takes a lot more than this hot weather to lay out an old war-horse like me," Mrs. Hudnut laughed contagiously, her salt-and-pepper shaded wig cocked dangerously nearer one ear than the other.

"My, how you keep your color, dearie. I couldn't help but notice Sarie Thatcher's girl, Ellen. She looks as peaked as a summer squash. I tell Sarie, she works Ella too hard. The work goes on with the precision of a canning factory. No wonder the girl is a wall-flower—too tired to sparkle. But ye can't tell Sarie anything. Sarie is all for the looks of things, not for the feeling. I'm scared to death to put my foot in her house—everything is so immaculate. I sometimes wish to the bottom of my shoes—she had more in her head!"

"Oh Elvira," cried Lucy gently, "don't be too hard on her. She is an excellent housekeeper and takes the prize at the fair on her salt-rising bread."

"Sure she does, Lucy, but I'll be blessed if I like to go there! They never have time for real living. For my part I'd rather see my man comfortable and happy even if there was a little dust—than to find me so cross from overwork he prefers to live in the corn-crib where I wasn't. But changing the subject, Lucy, did ye just ever see such a hot place as that Ladies Aid Society was the other day?"

"I didn't get to stay very long," answered Lucy, taking a jelly roll from the oven. "I had to come home to see about my chickens, I was afraid they would all drown in the storm."

"I thought I had as much right to express my mind as Mrs. Sharp and that coterie of hers. I'll be blessed, If I didn't up and say it too. I just took the bull by the horns and plunged in."

"Good for you, Elvira," agreed Lucy with enthusiasm, "but I'm sure I couldn't have done it."

"Well, you know, Lucy, how matters have stood in this neighborhood for years. There has never been anybody who dared express an opinion from cookin' to politics—

but what Grandma Shanks and her posterity either made it or broke it. Hope Middleton, that high falutin' granddaughter of her'n, actually had the nerve to infer that I was an old fogy—clear behind the procession, just because I didn't approve of their new Klan. It's just a pure money scheme to me."

"You are right there, Elvira," responded Lucy warmly, "I don't approve of it either, but of course everyone to his own opinion. If people would just work as hard in the church as they do for their lodges, they might git somewhere. I've always reasoned that by the time I gave the Lord a tenth of everything I had—my money, my time, my talents, and the like—I didn't have much time left for such things."

"A woman, by the time she raises her family and tends to them carefully, providing for their needs abundantly, ain't got no time to be gaddin' around huntin' up offices in such affairs—and that's just what I told 'em."

Then Elvira tossed her head a bit, until Becky almost stopped breathing for fear the wig, a salt-and-pepper affair, would lose its balance.

"But Elvira dear," said Lucy, worried like, "I suppose you realize just what you have done—cut yourself out of popular favor in the neighborhood until you will be left out in lots of ways! You will be along with us—we are considered queer and odd. We believe the human race to be all of God's dearly loved children, the Negroes included! We refuse to turn against the Jews for they are our Redeemer's chosen people—there is a curse pronounced upon all who do such things. You know, Elvira, God scattered the Jewish race because they rejected Christ and crucified Him, then our Heavenly Father pronounced a curse upon all those who would persecute them after they were scattered among the nations. As for our being against the Catholics, I will have no part in it for this is a free country. We believe in religious toleration, in other words, the free agency of man—so you see Elvira dear, I belong somewhere else not in that Klan."

"That sounds like purty straight religion to me," replied Elvira seriously, "It has lots of sense to it—I don't never intend to quarrel with you about your religion but I have my doubts about some of these here neighbors of ours."

"Don't worry about that, Aunt Elvira," Becky said gaily, "no doubt you are right but we don't expect people of the world to love us anymore than they did the early followers of our Savior. They killed them off as fast as they could in ancient times, but this dispensation of the gospel is not to fail as the others did, or rather wear out—because our Savior comes. We long and pray for His coming but it is foolish for us to expect everyone to listen—for all are not of the seed of Joseph."

27

"That last is about like Greek to me," answered Elvira bewildered "I--

The screen door on the side porch flew open--

"Bless my heart if here isn't my old sweetheart again." Wherewith Andy crossed the room in long strides and assisted the old lady to arise—gracefully whirled her away in an old-fashioned dance, gaily whistling the tune of the "Irish Washerwoman." Seeing that she was getting tired, he ended it all with a promenade, then led her back to her chair.

"You're the delight of my heart, Andy dear, it will be a sad day when I dance no more. Ye better be hurrying up with the wedding bells as I see me old legs is gettin' stiff."

"All signs fail in dry weather, Elvira," Lucy teased, "lately it has been very wet."

"Why are people in love like ostriches with their heads in the sand?" Becky queried with a wink at Andy.

"Gee-ma-nee, folks, so long! I must see how Grandpa is." Andy flushed dark red and tried to make a hurried exit.

"Wait a minute," called Elvira, "I'll go with you." She laughingly joined Andy on the stairs in the hall beyond the dining room.

Becky finished the downstairs work, while Lucy sat and read by the kitchen table. When Elvira returned she gave her the new tomato-pickle recipe and then walked down to the road with her old friend. Lucy had known Elvira for years—the longer she knew her the better she loved her.

Coming back up the lane alone to the house, Lucy looked at her old home. How well she remembered the day her husband, Robert, had lifted her over the door-sill, as a happy bride. The thought of those early years of happiness made her sigh without her realizing it. From the time he had been taken, life had held nothing much for her but fond hopes for children and sacred memories. Her mind had been turned to the Infinite by his going and she had suffered. There was no faith that had given her what she needed so desperately.

Despairingly, she had turned to reading her Bible, taking it literally for what ailed her. She was astonished to see the terrible difference between the Gospel as the early saints had taught it and the religion of modern Christianity. She decided that the difference was what was causing her trouble, and she began to pray to the Christ of the Bible for peace to overcome her sorrow.

The Lord became to her a Glorified Being, with a body of flesh and bones, the like of which she had—only made immortal through the power of the Resurrection. In her mind's eye she laid her head upon those blessed feet and cried in humility and anguish of soul for Him to assuage her grief and let her learn more of His holy will—that she might live a life of usefulness before Him. She acknowledged that the load was too heavy for her to bear and begged Him to take the matter into His own hands because it was crushing her.

Then it was that she heard "the still, small voice"—so sweet and tender—say unto her.

"You are my child, I will care for you. Be of good cheer–thy loved one liveth."

A few words, but who could ask for anything more? She was claimed and provided for—she was comforted through the spirit of Christ. From that hour she ceased to be a sectarian for she believed in modern revelation. Perhaps that was why she failed to follow the ministers when they spoke of the Resurrection as a spiritual affair altogether The Eternal Being who spoke to her, she knew, had a body as a man has and she believed that had her spiritual eyes been open, she would have seen Him in his glory near her. Without anyone telling her, she realized she existed as the butterfly in the cocoon, that creation leads to creation, there being no end to her Heavenly Father's works.

The weak discussions of so-called science no longer bothered her. She knew there was a Supreme Being who was "the same yesterday, today, and forever." From that time she ceased to question why Robert was taken from her, believing in some way that it was necessary. She began to live, rejoicing in her work and full of prayer and praise, content that it should be as it was. Thinking that way, she came to the realization that death led to the abundant life and she understood the saying of the Lord--

"The day of one's death is more precious in the sight of the Lord than the day of one's birth."

She thought too of her dear old father and was supremely thankful for him. Together often in the quiet evening their prayers for guidance ascended to the Holy One, full of praise and thanksgiving. Together they acknowledged His hand in all their ways.

Was it astonishing then that 'ere many days had passed, two strangers had come to their door, dusty, worn and weary, but eagerly anxious to answer questions after their mission was stated? To Lucy and her father it was the immediate answer to all their prayers—a fulfillment of the promise--

"Seek and ye shall find, knock and it shall be opened unto you."

The coming of these two young missionaries, and the acceptance of the Gospel as they taught it, entirely changed the whole of everything for Lucy and her father. They were content in life since they had found the source of all things and, like Cornelius of old, they were baptized after they had received the Holy Spirit.

Chapter 3 The Mastermind

Riversdale, like every city, had its political boss. The less he worked in daylight, so the good people of the community could know about it, the better. Such a man was John Manning: affable, well-poised in manner, secretive and designing in heart, he held matters much to his satisfaction. Recently, however, as a result of the combined efforts of public opinion, molded by the pulpit and press, he had felt some uneasiness with regard to his position.

He sat in his luxuriant office, a frowning expression upon his handsome features. The traffic in the street below did not attract him. He intently studied the papers in his hands, then shaking his head he arose and filed them away.

Taking his hat from its hook, he hurried into the hallway and made his way to the street below, where his handsome car awaited him. In a few seconds he was out of the city onto the quiet river road.

The morning air was sweet with the fragrance of clover. White clouds like fantastic floats sailed majestically in the bluest of blue skies. This drive on the north side of the river was, in the earliest times, an Indian trail. No doubt Tecumseh's braves had passed this way, under the gigantic sycamores on their march to defeat on the

Tippecanoe battleground under the command of the old Indian false-prophet. Sometimes, glimpses of aged farmhouses and barns with imposing silos could be seen from across the sparkling river, stationed high on the hills among the tall trees and undergrowth. These might easily bring to mind the romantic lover, in the setting of castles on the Rhine.

However, none of these beauties touched the heart of John Manning. Being a matter-of-fact businessman, his mind was not raised above the questions at hand. The poetry of nature was something quite ordinary to him, like a cup of coffee. He held himself in high esteem because he had been so successful in a lucrative way. Life to him was measured in such a manner, he had no room for the artistic or spiritual qualities with which some souls are so highly gifted. The governing rule of his life was to provide handsomely for John Manning and "the devil could look out for the rest."

Of course he was never satisfied, "the fields just over the fence" always appeared more delicious than the one he trod in. He wanted desperately to be happy. For twenty-five years, he had been expected to find that goal, but the myth was such a will-o'-the-wisp that it was impossible to catch up with her." He had no perspective of life as a whole, no philosophy. As a matter of fact, he was really nothing but a plebeian. At all times he was dressed elegantly and surrounded by luxury, but it was as impossible for him to become an aristocrat as for the moon to refuse to shine.

He drove expertly with his mind centered on his business alone. He saw the Madison place across the river but drove on until he came to the handsome new bridge which spanned the water near Clarksburg, then turned, crossed the bridge, and came east past the Pendelton home. Just before he reached the boundary of the Madison and Pendelton farms, he slowed down suddenly and turned his car out into the grass beside the road near the high wire fence. He got out of his car and stood in the hot sunshine waiting.

A man was plowing the field, following the plow with the lines thrown around his waist and guiding the plow with his hands. It was a difficult problem to tell which was the more angular and unkept, he or his sorrel horses. Manning hailed him as he turned the horses onto the furrow next to the road and watched him as he came toward him, a slight curl rested on Manning's lips. Both man and beast were sweating; the horses, wide-nostriled and grim, advanced to the soft clink of chain and strain of leather.

"Good morning, Ezra," said Manning pleasantly, "how is everything coming?"

"Perty fair," answered the farm-hand sourly, "jest middlin'."

Ezra had "Brung his old woman and little gals" from North Carolina some thirteen years before. Life never had held anything for him, and the probabilities were it never would. He was a true child of ignorance and poverty. He saw, with unmistakably greedy eyes, the prosperity of others and for some reason unknown to himself alone, he could not rise to their level, so his disposition became revengeful and cankered. At home he was hard to live with, taking out on his frail wife and children the effect of his discontent; when in the field that lot fell to the horses.

Manning motioned to Ezra to come closer to the fence and there they had been standing in a huddle for three-quarters of an hour when Charlotte found them.

She had been up to the woods to get the papers Andy left under the leafy burdock as he said he would. For camouflage reasons she came down on the Madison side of the fence in search of elderberries and was just starting to climb through a broken place in the hedge of berry bushes, when she saw Ezra Weeks standing there talking to the city man. Instinct told her their conversation was of a secret nature, that Mr. Manning did not care to be seen by anyone, and worst of all that somehow Andy and his family were involved. She knew

Ezra was a bitter and unrelenting enemy of Andy. Ever since Andy had forced Ezra to leave the maple logs that were too small, he had been cutting out of contract for himself on old Sister Wilson's farm the winter before. Ezra had at the time threatened to thrash Andy within an inch of his life but was merely laughed at and invited to come on. Like the true coward he was, Ezra had sneered and slouched away through the undergrowth of the woods to abide his time.

Charlotte also feared Manning, for she knew him to be a man to who treated business as business, and once someone fell into his power, there was no quarter. She recalled with a spasm of sorrow that Manning held the mortgage on the Madison home. Like a wild bird she drew back and hid herself in the elderberry shrubs, scared for fear she had already been seen. But of their conversation she could hear nothing.

At last Manning, after a final nod, stepped into his car and returned in the direction he came from. He was nearly out of sight by the time Ezra had yelled, "Giddap!" and resumed his plowing. Charlotte waited until this hired man of her father's was well down the furrow before she came out onto the river road. With Andy's pamphlets well hidden under the paper in the bottom of her basket of berries, she hurried home, perplexed and upset at heart for his sake.

When Charlotte got home, weary in body and mind, her sister Jane met her at the back kitchen door. Jane was fresh and immaculate, not a wave of her blond hair lay out of place, not a wrinkle of any kind in her delicate pink cotton voile dress. A sigh escaped Charlotte as she noticed all this.

Jane looked at Charlotte disapprovingly and gave her head an upward toss.

"This is a pretty time to be getting in, you've been gone hours," she spoke irritatingly. "Mother is dead tired. Mercy! Didn't you get anymore than that? I was going to help you clean them, but you have so few I don't think I need to bother!" She gave Charlotte another disdainful look and disappeared in the direction of the living room, where she began to play some of what she called "classy modern music."

Charlotte sighed again but this time with relief since Jane hadn't taken the basket. Her heart stood still at the thought of Jane finding Andy's Pamphlets in her possession. That would have been terrible.

As she went into the pantry and took down a big dishpan to turn her well-filled basket of berries into, a bitter thought crept unconsciously into her mind, of how dreadfully elderberries stain white hands. She saw them well-shaped and carefully manicured but brown, strong and capable looking. Unconsciously also, her chin lifted ever so slightly, with the thought of how many useful things these hands were trained to do. Not overbearing but respectfully, she thought of some obstacles they had overcome which character alone can accomplish. The stinging effect of Jane's manner and words faded. She thought with a deeply abiding love of her father. Of the many times he had taken her as a child on the plow to the field and there kept her the day through, answering her many questions gently and teaching her the nobility of honest labor.

"For," he had said to her one day, "Charlotte, there are kings and queens on this earth—some are crowned, some are not. The man or the woman who does their share in this life, laboring day after day—perhaps at duties they dislike, yet persisting through it all—they are the true kings and queens, my girl,"

Ever since that far off day she had been trying inch-by-inch, the best she knew how, to live up to the vision those words unfolded to her. Hence without bitterness toward life, she made up her mind to clean the elderberries, make the jelly, and think of peaceful things. Someday good would come to her. So the berries were turned quietly into the pan, the pamphlets were hidden in the pockets of her dress under her dainty apron, and she, unobserved, reached the quiet of her own room.

Knowing full well how often Jane went on the policy of "what is thine is mine" and that her room would be entered at any time during her absence, Charlotte carefully hid the papers far under her big rug and sat down for a bit to cool off.

After the heat of the glaring sun, this room was a haven of rest. She had painted the old-fashioned pieces of furniture and decorated them herself. It had taken a long time to collect them, but her bed was really a find. It had four moderately low posts evidently turned by a Dutchman who loved his drinks for on top of each bedpost rested a perfect goblet with the semblance of foam on it. She loved the heavy rolling pin at the foot and the plain beauty of the well-turned headboard. Her father had made the tasteful dressing table, which she had draped with a delicate flowered chintz, much like her bed. It was painted and decorated as the rest of her things, a rich ivory, and contained the reflection of two candlesticks with orange silk shades, edged in black and covered with hand-crocheted lace like her bedspread.

No one could count the hours of backbreaking labor it had taken to remove the old varnish from the few pieces of furniture she had collected, nor the amount of attention and pains that had gone into their decoration and the making of the many beautiful handmade things that the room contained. There was only one picture that hung in this simple room, with deep cream-toned walls, a flock of sheep coming home from the pasture with their shepherd, who carried tenderly in his arms a wee lamb.

The quiet and peace of this little sanctuary of her own, fell like soothing balm upon Charlotte and she leaned back and relaxed in her deep wing chair. She looked out her broad open window where a gentle breeze waved the simple stenciled curtains and saw a couple of bees toying among the pink and white geraniums growing in the luxuriantly filled flower box. Before she realized what had happened, she had lost consciousness.

With a start Charlotte awoke to find Aunt Em standing in her doorway.

"Land sakes, Charlotte Pendelton, wake up Ye air sleepin' like the dead!" Aunt Em was breathing loudly with asthma and the effect of climbing the stairs. "It beats me how young folks kin sleep. Here I am—layin' awake night after night, can't stand it till morning. Did ye know it was nearly evenin'?

"It must have been the effect of my walk in the fresh air and sun," Charlotte explained laughingly. She quickly stood up before her aunt.

"Bless my heart, child, but ye sure air growin' up, look jest like yer Ma when she was young." Aunt Em's voice was full of love. "You must be careful and never give her reason to grieve, dearie."

Charlotte slipped her arms around this gentle old aunt, who though at times did not understand her, nevertheless truly loved her. She buried her face in her ample bosom and asked Aunt Em if she needed any help with the cooking.

"You jest know I do, that sky-larkin' Jane has a dinner date here with that John Manning's son and we are to put our best foot forward—so I've been given to understand dearie."

"Not Cecil?" queried Charlotte astonished.

"That's the identical feller, honey, ain't that grand?"

"I don't like him, Aunt Em," said Charlotte as they went downstairs.

"That will just suit Jane fine, dearie! Now you get the best things out and arrange the asters in the silver bowl like Jane told me to tell you to do. There's a big dance at the country club soon and Jane is fishin' for a date. So help her out, will ye?"

Aunt Em bustled off to the kitchen to finish the chicken pie, make the salad and season the vegetables properly.

Charlotte did as she was bidden with little relish for the thought that Cecil Manning was coming. She knew they were in reality but simple farm-folk. It did not look well for them to be mingling with high society people, in her mind, and in some way she was distrustful. She looked up and saw her sister standing beneath the arch in the sitting room. Jane was dressed like a beautiful Dresden doll, in a simple pale pink satin gown of the sheerest of net. She wore Charlotte's exquisite strand of crystals. As usual, she looked coldly from her icy blue eyes and snapped—

"For the love of heaven, Charlotte, go get some decent clothes on! I do wish you would show a little more discretion in what you wear and where you wear it. A dress like that is for morning wear only!"

"Charlotte knew that Jane was in a tense mood and was determined not to be thwarted. For that matter, what she said was law in the household, everybody was marshaled behind her, except Charlotte and her father, and even they let things go as a rule rather than have trouble with her.

So Charlotte left Jane overlooking her work and returned to her own room. She thought about the new dress that Jane had purchased for the evening and how because of her extravagance she must wear again the already well worn evening gown she had of green crepe-de-chine with its now almost shabby slippers to match. This gown she had received from Aunt Em to wear to the Junior Prom in her last year in high school. It never occurred to her to go into Jane's elegantly furnished French bedroom and appropriate one of the many delicate frocks hanging in her closet.

Charlotte quickly arranged her hair and donned the worn dress. She thought of how Jane was needlessly running her worried father into debt just for clothes which half the time she disdained. Unashamed, she calmly looked herself over in the mirror. She was a well-formed young woman inclined to slenderness, crowned by an abundant wealth of wavy black hair. Her large, gentle gray eyes, framed by delicately arched brows, took in the sight of her perfectly straight nose, clear complexion with a soft pink hue, and her pearl-white teeth set between naturally red lips. She wore no jewelry and did not care if it was so.

"Anyhow," she whispered to herself thoughtfully, "Andy loves me and I love him, so I'm not going to worry about other things."

Had she but realized it, she was very elegantly dressed, for she dominated her gown with a lovely personality, unneeded by anything more to make her an attractive girl.

The important guest arrived promptly and every detail of the evening passed as planned. Leander had been marshaled off to spend the evening at Ezra's lowly home. Jane did not intend to run even the risk of anything he might say or do.

"I'd be ashamed to have him around here, Mother, with those warts all over his hands."

So Cora meekly consented to his going, thinking of the time when Jane might be married.

Charlotte felt sad all through the dinner. Where did she have anything in common with this scheme of her mother's? She knew her father did not approve of either Manning or his son. She was glad when the meal was finished so she might escape to the kitchen and help with the dishes. Charlotte did not like Cecil Manning even to a small degree.

"He is entirely too bold with his actions and his eyes. Besides he takes everything as though he was entitled to it and never seems to think what effort might lie behind it."

Before long, Jane left in Cecil's fast sports-roadster. Weary and lonely in heart, Charlotte went up to her room to think and read. As it was but dusk she did not turn on her light, but rested idly in the big wing chair by the open window with Andy's pamphlets in her lap. She could see in the dim light the title of the first article, "Why I Believe in Mormonism" by Dr. Charles W. Penrose. The subject took her fancy but at the same time she hesitated to turn on her light and read.

Some unseen personage or cautious bit of reason seemed to say to her--

"You had better not read this stuff. Why not let Andy think you read it and you really won't have to bother with it. Don't you know that the Mormons are talked about everywhere? Surely where there is so much smoke there is some fire. Why not be satisfied with what you have and not bring a lot of heartache and trouble into your life? You know very well that even your dear father won't understand this and you will just make an outcast of yourself from your family. Look at the Madisons, no one really has much to do with them, they are considered too queer for any use. Why be like them? One should not deliberately make life hard and that is exactly what you would be doing if you read these articles and believed them. You had better tell Andy that religion is a matter of personal choice and that you do not care to be deeply involved in religion in your life. The really intelligent people do not think too deeply nor ponder long on mysteries; no one can fathom mysteries, it is not meant that the human race should understand!"

Charlotte decided quickly that lying about reading the pamphlets would only lead to exposure and that would be an ordeal to bear. And anyhow, she did not like to deceive anyone about anything.

"If you can't read this pamphlet, Charlotte Pendelton, and use your own judgment about matters, I pity you! What are you anyway—a little jelly-fish that can't use her own head?"

She reached for the cord and turned on the shaded lamp beside her chair, then picked up the article. It seemed a foreign thing in her hands. Somehow she did not want anyone to catch her reading. She rather blushed to herself.

"You silly goose," she murmured, "don't you know that Andy and Becky Madison are both ardent Mormons? Now just where have you met nicer people? Are they not refined and more cultured and well-read than any of the rest of the young people around you?"

Charlotte had to admit that there was not another the equal of the two in the neighborhood nor had she met any such in Riversdale. They evidently lived for a purpose.

"I wonder if it is the effect of the religious training their mother has given them? If it is, it must be a wonderful religion to accomplish the results it has." With a stubborn will which drowned every whit of cautious reason, she picked up the forbidden article and began to read with an open mind.

Charlotte did not notice the way time flew while she was reading. Before she laid the article down, it had been read twice.

"This Dr. Penrose," she began to reason to herself, "is an accomplished writer, or else he is gifted with a power and authority I never met in any writer before. The way he explains things is perfectly amazing. Why, he actually tells me I have to repent and be baptized again before I can ever enter the Kingdom of Heaven. He calls all ministers "false teachers" because he says they preach a gospel different from what Paul preached. It is terrible. I don't believe it. I don't believe it!"

Through the white heat at the injustice, as she saw it, of the author's remarks a single question came to her.

"Dr. Penrose says, and you know yourself, that your Bible says that Christ organized His church and then gave gifts unto them. Now where in your church are the gifts?"

"O dear, I don't know," she wailed to her own heart. "We don't believe in revelation anymore from the Lord like the prophets of old and His disciples knew it, and we don't have miracles anymore. I reckon the gifts He gave must have been tossed overboard along with the other things, too."

With a start she realized she was brought face-to-face with Becky's explanation in the last Sunday School class and she remembered the statement about the modern churches being without the proper authority invested in their leaders and flock.

"Dr. Penrose says," she repeated slowly, "the whole present plan of modern Christianity is like that of a tree. If the trunk is without authority to perform the needed ordinances for membership in Christ's kingdom, even so then, are the limbs and twigs. Christ's doctrine is not one of confusion but one that leads to the unity of the faith, even as Christ was one in unity with the Father's will, so we should be one in the will of Christ."

Charlotte had read and reread her ancient history and her mind easily turned to the Roman arenas and then to the later scenes of the so-called Dark Ages. She had often wondered why those centuries were called the Dark Ages. With Dr. Penrose's explanation of the absence of the Priesthood from the earth during those centuries, light began to filter through, and she saw why it was so called and understood the literal fulfillment of Peter's prophecy of the apostasy that was to come.

"If I read anymore of this literature," she murmured uneasily, "I'm going to be terribly unhappy. I might have known it, but surely I can think and reason until I see whether the Truth is here or not. But, if you do see the Truth, Charlotte Pendelton, and it isn't what you want to see at all, what are you going to do about it? Will you have the courage to follow it?"

If Charlotte entered her room sad in spirit, she was none the happier now. She felt like the rich young man who came to Christ and asked what he should do to be saved. She remembered with a sigh, how Jesus had told him to go and sell all that he had, and give it to the poor, then come and follow Him. It was, in other words, "Pick up your cross and follow me."

"Sara Thatcher says," whispered Charlotte, thinking deeply, "there isn't any cross now for Christians to carry, because everyone around us knows about the gospel and there are no days of persecution any longer." Yet, she reasoned, "Christ says himself that all who would come after Him should suffer persecution. Well, all I have to say is that if I believe this man's words, I will undoubtedly suffer a little myself. I'd have to give up not as much maybe as the rich young Jew but all the same it would be everything in life I hold dear—except Andy."

"Oh dear," she cried miserably, "why did I ever let myself begin to read anyway. I should have told Andy we could never be married in the first place."

With a misery the depth and like of which she had never known before, she laid the articles again under her rug and turned to her chair to put out her light.

Wondering what a scrap of white paper lying on the floor might be, she stopped and picked it up. It was a letter written on very thin notepaper, her very first love letter, and from the man she was seriously beginning to wonder if she could completely remove him from her heart.

The letter told her everything that a man who truly loves always tells his beloved. It brought tears of tenderness to Charlotte's eyes. Her heart, that she had resolved to begin to shield with a wall of ice, burned with a greater flame than ever at the realization that this was his letter to her. She forgot home, mother, father, and all dear associations and longed to be as Andy wished her in life- -a helpmate to him. She remembered what God had said about man and wife, how they should be one flesh and cleave unto each other, through all of life with its trials.

The letter ended with an invitation to a little picnic party the following evening.

Well along in the night, Charlotte awoke and began to ponder again the question which bothered her. Could she follow the Truth if she came to the conclusion Andy's church was right? Hadn't she better give Andy up after all? Even Andy might be wrong, he had never been "out West" to see for himself. What did he know about it? It might be quite different out there, than things sounded on paper.

"This is a deceitful old world," she reasoned, "I think it best to give him up. Yet I love him, and if I can't marry him I don't want to marry anybody. That is a really beautiful way that he looks on marriage, as something which death does not close nor the glory to beauty of it ever fade. I like that, but oh dear, this authority business is hard to swallow–anyhow there is one redeeming feature about it. Dr. Penrose doesn't think the ministers are aware of their position—but blinded—so I reckon it may be said he is after all charitable to them. I won't break off right away with Andy, I'll study a little more, then too, I must kinda look out for him and this Ezra Week's business."

With crisscross thoughts still persisting in her mind, Charlotte could come to no immediate decision. She finally drifted into sleep again to awaken with early dawn.

Chapter 4 Doctor Stone

"Let's see now," began Becky, "it says two cups of sugar, one cup of water, three tablespoons cinnamon drops, one teaspoon red cake coloring and six apples." Becky quickly got out the saucepan for the syrup and began to core and quarter the large red apples from their orchard. She wore a fresh blue and a white gingham dress adorned by a jaunty red bow sash. Her black curls bobbed energetically as she worked.

"I expect I'd better make that recipe double for such healthy farm appetites." She spoke softly to herself, totally unaware of a tall gentleman at the porch screen-door.

"I beg your pardon," he said, "but is this where Madisons live?"

Becky, rather surprised, advanced quickly to the door, grasping a paring knife in one hand and a red apple, from which half the curled peeling dangled, in the other. She realized she was in the presence of rather a handsome stranger—a person of refinement and perhaps sophistication.

"Why yes, it is," answered Becky, suddenly aware of the homely paring knife and the dangling apple peeling. She did not know that she made a very charming picture.

"Is Andrew Madison at home today?"

"Yes sir, he is at the barn. Shall I call him for you?"

"Never mind, I will step out there myself," he said pleasantly and tipped his hat.

"It is so near eleven o'clock I'll venture that man is here for lunch," Becky thought to herself as she turned back to her cooking. She flew around quickly and put the apples in the oven, then prepared an extra amount of vegetables for the guest. "Andy is always doing that and I'd better be ready."

Lucy came downstairs from caring for her father, and noticed the added sparkle in Becky's manner. She was curious but said nothing.

After awhile in rather a shy way, Becky said—

"Mother dear, there is a gentleman at the barn talking to Andy. I thought no doubt Andy would ask him to lunch. May we have the table fixed on the porch today?"

"That would be lovely, dear, if I meet him I'll ask him to stay if Andy hasn't. Use the blue dishes, if you like, and the white lattice basket for the flowers."

Andy soon returned to the kitchen with the gentleman. Becky had spread out the leaves to the old black walnut drop-leaf table and laid two runners at right angles across its waxed surface. In its center she placed the white basket full of English pinks. She then laid the lovely old blue-willow dishes.

"Mother darling," exclaimed Andy, "I want you to meet my dear old friend, Dr. Douglas Stone. He is here passing through to Michigan on his vacation."

"I am delighted to meet you, Doctor. I have heard Andy speak so much of you."

"My sister, Becky—Dr. Stone," Andy said proudly.

"Miss Becky," responded the doctor graciously, "how does it come I've never heard you speak of your sister, Andy?"

"Well, those were pretty busy days at Purdue, Doctor. But now that you are here, why not make us that little visit you've promised me so long?"

"That would be fine, Doctor," said Lucy, "If you can possibly stay, it would be such a pleasure to have you— for Andy especially."

"I will not take 'No' for an answer, Doctor Stone," laughed Andy good naturedly. "Sis here is an awful good cook and I'm sure it's much better than that found in restaurants."

Doctor Stone smiled and said, "Well, since you wish me to remain with you, I guess I could cut a week off that hunting and fishing trip. I always did want to come to see you and meet your people—now I'm here, I like the place, and if you don't mind my saying so, I'm charmed at the invitation's prospects."

"Just take the doctor to the east room upstairs then Andy, and, Doctor, I want you to make yourself at home. We as a rule rise early and retire the same way. If you can be happy with us, we will be delighted to have you stay as long as you can."

"Thank you, Mrs. Madison," said the Doctor.

Doctor Stone followed Andy into the wide front hall that opened onto the back screened-porch, then up the spacious open stairway. Father Mahoney's door was open, so Andy peeped in—the old gentleman was awake.

"Grandfather dear, may we come in?"

"Shure and ye can!"

Smiling, Andy turned to Dr. Stone. "Come," he said and they entered the invalid's room.

"I want you to meet Dr. Stone, Grandfather. He is here as our guest for a week at least."

"Tis a pleasure indade to meet ye—faith and ye air the fione man Andy is always telling me about, I don't care if ye didn't come from ould Ireland. Sometimes I think it a pity I iver come over, but begorra then I think I ought to be ashamed of meself."

Grandfather's white hands raised warmly to greet him and took the doctor's brown one.

"I hope ye will be plazed wid the time spent wid us."

"I am sure I will," the doctor's eyes twinkled.

"Air ye double or single?"

"I'm single," laughed the doctor delightedly.

"Oh my, that's a bad loife for the likes of ye 'ter be livin'."

"But it is an awful fact," lamented the doctor shaking his head sadly—"an awful fact!"

"Indade it is. Couldn't no girls iver luv ye?"

"I've never found the right one," roared the Doctor.

"Och, Oil'll niver belave ye—niver!" Grandfather's head rolled in merriment on the pillows. "When I wuzyer age—begorra, Oi had thet question all sittled myself. Oi had locked up me girl's warm heart close to mine furiver and thin we lost the key."

"We will come up again, Grandfather," laughed Andy gaily, "we mustn't tire you out. Come with me, Doctor, and I'll show you to your room." Andy crossed the hall and opened the door directly opposite Grandfather's.

It has been years since Doctor Stone had stepped into a room like this. He had a feeling as if he had arrived home after many years of weary wandering. He was suddenly carried back to the days of childhood in the sunny southland. He could almost hear Mammy Chloe singing in the backyard as of 'yore. Everything was so old-fashioned, just like Father Mahoney's room but this was nicer still, more livable and feminine. Andy closed the door and left him.

As Dr. Stone came downstairs, he passed Becky taking up a tray to her grandfather. He thought her rather shy and distant but he was used to girls who were just the opposite. He noticed the delicate whiteness of her skin and the utterly reckless way the little black curls clung to her forehead in perspiration. He was genuinely pleased to be a guest in this delightful old home and promptly told Lucy so when he joined her with Andy at the table.

"Well, that is nice of you to say so," responded Lucy, arranging the quaint teacups. "Most people nowadays don't like old things; they think one is kinda queer if they do. But there is so much dear association with my things that I somehow dislike parting with them."

"It is a shame that we furnish our houses as we do. We are like so many sheep; what one does the other must do also. Our houses should reflect our personalities, and I like to see the differences," Dr. Stone spoke warmly.

"I like that way of thinking too," said Andy. "I tell Mother here, this is the dearest home in the world. There is not a thing in it we don't use or that is too nice to use."

"Andy dear," smiled Lucy, "I appreciate that remark. This is an old-fashioned place, but it suits me. I am hopelessly that way myself. Let us live, dear, in the hope that fashion will revert to former days, then all will be well again. What do you want to venture that it won't be three years until long evening dresses and furbelows will come in again?"

"Gee, that would be queer, Mother," laughed Andy. "How do you think you'd like that, Doctor?"

"Oh, I don't know, but I think I'd rather like it. But you never can tell what the ladies will do—look what happened to them right after the war."

Becky returned and seated herself. After a short blessing was asked, they began to eat. The meal was delicious. There was tender sliced cold ham, baked potatoes, new peas with tiny tender carrots, tomato salad, baked apples, rich brown bread, and fresh raspberries with little tea cakes.

"Mother dear, I believe I'd better have my hogs vaccinated and if Doctor Stone does not mind, I'd rather he did the job than that doctor we've had from Riversdale. I might be able to get a few friends to join in as well, if the doctor is willing."

"I would be happy to do the job for you, Andy. Anything I can help you with, I will be only too glad to do it."

"If you want me to, I might help you make a few more dollars anyway, Doctor. This neighbor-hood is all scared of the cholera, and Dr. Price is so busy in the northern part of the county. We are all afraid he will not be able to get to us in time."

"If that's the case, Andy, it becomes my duty to take off my vacation-coat and go to work. I never got much thrill out of vacation anyhow. I'm glad I came now, if for no other reason than just because I'm needed."

"He has not met any of the people in the neighborhood, Becky," said Andy. "Why can't we give a little neighborhood party and make him acquainted. Instead of that little picnic we planned for tonight, let's have the party tomorrow night."

"Oh no," began the doctor, "that will be too much trouble."

"Not at all," said Andy gaily, "will it, Sis? Becky turns off parties like a boy does hand-springs. She bosses and I help."

"I consent then," smiled the doctor, straight at Becky, "if you will let me have an apron and help too."

"Very well then," rejoined Becky gaily, "you can help turn the freezer to make the ice cream and lemon sherbet."

"Really?" Dr. Stone was grinning like a little boy.

"Really," answered Becky with sparkling eyes, "and if you don't do it right, shall I make you do it over again?"

Lucy's heart missed a beat or two at the arch little way Becky had asked the question. She looked at Andy to see if he could read between the lines, but that young rogue was evidently enjoying himself, and did not look at her. Lucy almost thought he did so on purpose.

They arose from the table. Andy reached over and drew Becky close to him.

"See here, Sis," he said teasingly, "help a poor fellow out—just slip over and tell my girl the change in the plans, will you? And be sure you tell her Pa and Ma to come along. It's time they find out what a nice fellow I really am."

"And if she wants to bring one of those rich devil food cakes of hers, what shall I say, darling?" bantered Becky.

"Tell her that the way to a young Irishman's heart always lies in that precise direction."

Andy and Dr. Stone went away to the barn and Becky, left with her mother, prevailed on the delicate lady to go lie down while she finished the dishes. She then departed for Charlotte's home.

62

Charlotte came to the door, she was deep in the art of making more elderberry jelly. Mr. Pendelton came into the kitchen for a snack of bread and new jelly.

Leander spoke up quickly with his mouth already full.

"You kin mop yer forehead, if ye want too, Pa, with red bandanna handkerchiefs but I stick my head under the pump."

"So I see, young man, but I'd sooner take a swim in the river. It's better for me, that way I cool off even."

"We are going to have a neighborhood party tomorrow night, so come over, Mr. Pendelton, and bring all the family. We'll have plenty of cold drinks and ice cream," Becky said.

Cora and Aunt Em came into the kitchen just in time to hear Becky's invitation.

"Law me, are you here, Becky Madison?" said Aunt Em sociably. "You're going to give a party? Do tell!"

"Yes, and we want you all to come," said Becky kindly.

"I don't know as we can very well," began Cora dryly, "we've been running around so much lately. It ain't likely we will. We need the sleep."

63

"Sleep, my eye," scoffed Tom Pendelton. "That's all I do—eat, work, and sleep. If you don't think you'll go, Ma, Charlotte, Leander, and I'll go. Won't we, Leander?"

"Little peas and buttonhooks," he gasped between mouthfuls, "Yes!"

When Becky departed, Charlotte followed her down to the road. Cora Pendelton, in the house, turned on Tom indignantly.

"Tom Pendelton, where is your head? Can't you see how the land lays? I for one am not anxious to go—they are just not our kind of folks!"

Tom Pendelton's eyes twinkled. "What's the matter, Ma, ain't they able to trace their grand-daddies back to the Revolution fer enough?

"For pity sake's, Tom Pendelton, behave yourself!" Cora stood with arms akimbo, staunch as an oak.

"Oh well, Corie," said Aunt Em soothingly, "It really has been a long while since we went to a neighborhood party. Let's go, once hadn't ought to hurt nuthin'."

"That's you, Em, all over. You are always and forever spoiling the men."

"I certainly hope Andy totes a keen violin tomorrow night." Tom winked broadly at Leander.

"I don't," snapped Cora.

"I hope they dance the 'Virginia Reel' and the 'Irish Washerwoman.' It's been a long time since I've seen a real dance."

"Don't talk anymore, Tom Pendelton. You never did have any religion. The example you're a settin' is terrible."

"The only trouble with dancing with you, Corie," said Tom acidly, "is you're too darn heavy. I took the yardstick t'other day and measured your hips and they was exactly thirty-six inches across!"

"You are a terrible exaggerator, Tom," cried Cora weakly, the tears beginning to come, "a terrible exaggerator! I don't want to go, but now I've got to or it would look queer."

Down at the end of Pendelton's lane, Charlotte and Becky stood talking. "How come it is a party instead of a picnic?" asked Charlotte eyes alight.

"Andy planned it because we have a doctor staying a few days with us."

"A medical doctor?"

"No, a hog doctor, a veterinarian!"

"Oh, oh," teased Charlotte, "someone new?" Shall I bring one of my cakes to help you out?

Then Becky told Charlotte what Andy had said.

"Did he really say that?" Charlotte blushed.

"Yes, he did, and we are all tickled pink."

"I am so happy, then," sighed Charlotte tenderly. "I want you all to love me, Becky, but oh dear, there is one thing that bothers me terribly, and it is this religion business."

"Don't worry about that dear, take your time and study things out. Have you a Book of Mormon?"

"No."

"Then I'll give you mine and you can read it and do just like it says to do. Ask Heavenly Father to let you know whether it is the Truth or not. I am sure that is the only thing that counts anyway."

Becky soon reached home and began to call the neighbors on the telephone. Every one promised to come, but none were so cordial as Elvira.

"Of course I'll come, honey," replied the old lady delightedly. "I'll bring my good-for-nothing bachelor-sons along and if you just say the word, a white layer cake."

"Bless your heart, Aunt Elvira, you know my weakness, don't you?"

"Well, considerin' the success of 'em cakes 'o mine, dearie, you ain't the only one with a weakness."

"Will it be a pineapple filling this time," teased Becky gaily.

"Of course it will, dearie, and the best I can make at that!"

"Aunt Elvira, what a blessing you are—I'll depend on you then."

Becky had just hung up the telephone when Andy with Dr. Stone came into the kitchen. They had been to

Riversdale to get the doctor's satchels. After they had carried them to the doctor's room, they came down to the kitchen and found Becky and her mother making angel food cakes as their share for the entertainment.

"Andy dear," signed Becky, between vigorous rounds of beating the egg whites, into a stiff froth, "we are making two cakes and two more are promised."

"You needn't tell me who did it—I know already," smiled Andy. "They are a type of people found once in a blue moon. God bless 'em."

"What made you think so?" asked Dr. Stone curiously. "I find a great many kindhearted people in this world."

"So do I," replied Andy quickly, "but very few who have the blood of Israel in their veins."

"Why, Andy?" questioned Lucy immediately, "who told you so?"

"I saw Elder Thorensen in town today, Mother dear. We were talking about things here and about our friends. He told me so and said to abide here a while, then come 'out west'-- that the time was short for us, but we were not to come alone."

"Will he be here to see us?" asked Becky shyly.

"In a few days, he said. He is located at the Indiana Hotel. If we wish to reach him any time, we can call there. He is quite busy with an Elder Barton."

"How nice that is—we must have them out here," said Lucy earnestly. "I am so weary to visit with someone of my faith."

Dr. Stone stood quite still watching them as they were grouped around the kitchen table. He was aware that for the time at hand he was quite out of their minds and they were discussing something they loved very much—but which was a complete mystery to him. It made him feel rather out of things and he sensed a difference he had not hitherto felt between himself and these people.

"Forgive me, Dr. Stone, for talking of strangers before you," exclaimed Lucy graciously. "But this is a dear old friend we have known and written to for years. Someday I hope you will have the pleasure of meeting him."

"He certainly is," asserted Andy vigorously. "He is a mighty man when it comes to preaching the Gospel, and does he do it."

"Like Paul, son—like Paul—for he is sometimes driven from place to place."

"I know, Mother, but I don't think it is as bad as it used to be that way. People now are just indifferent to any religion."

"What kind of doctrine does he preach then?" queried Dr. Stone. "I thought the days of persecution were past."

"He preaches Christ and Him crucified!" said Andy. "He preaches as few Latter Day Saints are blessed to preach for it is his special gift."

"Latter-Day Saints—why that's the Mormons, isn't it?" asked Dr. Stone. He hoped he didn't sound too surprised.

"Yes," said Lucy, "we are the only family of Mormons around here."

"I've never had the privilege of meeting any of your church before," replied the Doctor. "All my life I have left the field of religion alone. I was never much impressed, but I have often wondered what these Mormons preached that the others were so stirred up about."

"If that is the case then," said Lucy kindly, "in a few days I will give you a chance to talk to a real 'dyed-in-the-wool' Mormon elder. You will find him a very intelligent man and one you will always remember with pleasure."

"Won't Grandpa be glad to see him again," said Becky delightedly, pouring the new thoroughly sugared and floured egg-whites into the cake pan. "They are such dear friends."

"That will be a pleasure," said the Doctor, "I have always been curious about Mormons, but I don't promise to accept his teachings. In other words, I have to be shown."

"Then, my dear fellow," laughed Andy, "prepare to meet your Waterloo—that is, if you are open-minded and not prejudiced."

"If I see what he sees," said the Doctor seriously, "I can take it and stay with it—but if I don't, please don't expect me to change my views."

The doctor looked up, still in a reflective mood, and found Becky looking straight at him. There was something in her eyes he had not seen before. They looked at him intently, thoughtfully, seriously, completely wrapped in the possibilities of the statement he had made. Before he realized what he was doing, he was answering her word for word in the same silent sort of way, steadfastly and earnestly. They seem to reach an understanding because it was Becky who first sensed the situation and looked away with a slow dull blush. Dr. Stone's pulses stirred and suddenly Father Mahoney's words rang dizzily in his ears--

"Och, I'll never belave ye—niver!"

Chapter 5 a party instead of a picnic

"There now I'm sure the sherbet is done by now, Andy. Please put the freezer in the pantry," said Becky lightly. "You must be very tired from all that turning, Dr. Stone. Isn't this a fine way to treat a guest of honor?"

"I'm having fun on top of fun, let me assure you," returned the doctor, surveying his long white apron. "I am afraid this bit of protection is just about ruined though. Andy, did you get the teaspoons like she told you to?"

"I did, yer honor, and they're reposing in quiet dignity on the yonder pantry shelf. What is the next task it is our duty to perform?"

"Andy Madison," said Becky archly, "don't be silly—just hang those Japanese lanterns on the living room porch and be sure you don't fall off that wiggley old step-ladder."

"It's getting kinda late, Sis, maybe while I do this and get the jars out to put the flowers in, you had better go out to the garden and get those gladiolas. Maybe Dr. Stone could help you too."

"See that you get out a lot of vases then, Andy, as I don't like a stingy arrangement of flowers over the house."

Becky disappeared in the direction of the kitchen and returned with two big flower baskets and the scissors--

"Come this way, Doctor," she said.

By the time Andy had finished hanging the lanterns and found the vases, Becky and the doctor had returned, laden with the long-stemmed gladiolas, together with plenty of fern that grew along the north side of the house. They quickly put them on the kitchen table, got fresh water and filled the wide mouthed vases.

"I think there is just about every shade I can think of here," said the doctor, admiring the large lily-like stalks.

"They are Grandfather's favorite flower," said Becky. "He says people ought to be like them—for no matter if they are cut early—they fulfill their mission in spite of everything."

"I wish we were going to have him with us tonight—for a little while at least," said Dr. Stone.

"When we are done here, Andy dear, see if Grandfather would like to come down. I will put this biggest bowl of flowers on the low table by his couch. See, I thought perhaps we could bring him down and I've brought out a lot of pillows and Grandmother's old coverlet."

"Sure and he will want to come, I expect I'd better tend to that now—we're all done so I'll go up now and ask him."

Andy disappeared up the stairway and soon returned with the frail old gentleman in his arms, who was quite happy over the prospects of the evening. Andy gently laid him on the couch and covered him. His white beard and hair shone like silver against the pillows. Dr. Stone could not help but be shocked at his extreme thinness.

"Faith," exclaimed Grandfather jovially, "and this is a foine evening' fer the fairies to be out! I use ter think they wuz all left behind me in the ould country—but I belave I must 'uve been wrong, this is such a charmin' spot and we already have one fairy."

"I see what you mean, Grandfather darling," laughed Becky gaily. "You are always giving perfect evidence that you once hung out the window and kissed that famous Blarney stone—but let me assure you, these will be the substantial kind of fairies here tonight."

"Substantial in sight and form, yes," twinkled Grandfather, "but not in whim, Oh Lor' no—Oi use ter belave I wuz getting' along in a kinda substantial way with my girl, but belave me, I soon woke up an I didn't have ter pinch meself either to realize I'd been dreaming."

"Are they that difficult?" groaned Dr. Stone roguishly to Grandfather.

"They are so consarned, hard to nab, son—they kape yer dizzy, but thet is whut makes the game excitin'!"

"Well, I guess I'd better be trying then," teased the doctor, with laughing eyes on Becky.

Becky's cheeks grew a shade pinker as she turned to Grandfather. That old mischief was lying there on the couch, laughing silently and heartily to himself.

"I think it is time we had a little supper. You get your chores done, Andy," exclaimed Becky, business-like. "It won't be long before our guests begin to come and we have to get ready yet. Let's not wake Mother until everything is prepared."

Soon everything was ready and they were all assembled. Grandfather Mahoney returned thanks and then Becky gave him his tray.

"Oh, Mother, look someone is coming already."

Everyone turned to look toward the lane. There, sure enough, was a car turning in.

"Don't you know who that is?" exclaimed Andy joyously. "Why, Mother, it's Elder Thorensen, himself, and that must be Elder Barton with him!"

The family was eager to greet their old friends and trooped around them from the yard gate to the vine-clad porch.

"You are just in time, folks, to meet one of Andy's school friends - Dr. Stone - Elder Barton, Dr. Stone." Lucy introduced them happily.

"Are you a medical doctor?" asked Elder Thorensen kindly.

"No sir, I'm a veterinarian."

"Oh so, that is a wonderful thing," exclaimed Thorensen, "I am a doctor too, but a doctor that never gives pills or uses hypodermics. We are the doctors of souls, pointing the way – the patients must do the rest."

"That is interesting – Grandfather Mahoney here is an ardent admirer of your method," returned Doctor Stone graciously.

While Thorensen greeted Grandfather with real love and affection and introduced his companion, Becky and her mother laid fresh plates and prepared to entertain their new guests.

"We will excuse yez," said Grandfather to Andy and the Doctor. "Run along wid ye and get ready fer the gay doin's. I will entertain the elders, talkin'."

"What! Are we intruding on a party?" cried Thorensen, "Barton, perhaps we had better come another day."

"By no means, we'd love to have you stay," said Lucy. "Come, sit and eat. Everything is here and, if you will excuse us, we will get ready. Andy, take the gentlemen to the guest room back of Dr. Stone's."

Becky and Lucy hurried away, and Andy took his old friends to their room to prepare for their supper. Doctor Stone wandered out to the barn and began to help finish the chores. Andy joined him soon and together they finished up. When they returned to the house, the Elders were eating and chatting easily with Grandfather.

"Hurry ape," admonished Grandfather, "er some 'o 'em fairies we wuz talkin' about will be catchin' ye—in 'em overalls."

Upstairs, Dr. Stone stopped to rest a bit in the wide rocker by the open window. The breeze came in gently, fanning the dainty ruffled curtains.

"Of all the queer dear places," he murmured to himself, "this is the queerest and dearest. Here I am falling head-over-heels in love with a Mormon girl, in the state of Indiana. I thought they were all confined to Utah, and were only half-civilized—but believe me, I'm beginning to think that the more I find out about the Mormons the more I am going to respect them—or else these people would never have taken up with such a faith."

He gazed meditatively out upon the slow current of the river. It was beautiful and peaceful. He wished his life could always be laid in such pleasant places. The sign of a whippoorwill came echoing through the gathering twilight. It awoke a tender minor chord within his heart that played in pathos upon his soul.

"She is the most beautiful woman I have ever seen—born to be the heart of my heart and knit to my soul. I'm not half worthy of her, and Douglas Stone, I'll bet my last picayune she won't have you either."

Dr. Stone began to get ready for the evening. He bathed carefully and donned his suit of dark broadcloth. He wore a handsome white silk tie with his white shirt and a pair of dress shoes.

"I do wish you were better looking, old boy," he said to himself as he surveyed his reflection in the mirror from head to toe. "You are tall enough, and broad enough through the shoulders, thank the gods you are not fat—but I do wish your face wasn't so thin."

Dr. Stone had never worried over his looks before. He failed to realize that he was really a very handsome man with his fine high forehead and black waving hair—or that his eyes, although deep set, were large and of a very rare shade of warm brown. His nose was straight and his lips were set—he examined his smooth square chin to see if he had a perfect shave.

"You will have to do now. Alas, you can't change what Nature gave you, but--" he added, knitting his black brows, "if you had known what she was like, you might have made some improvements."

He met the other young folks in the hall below.

Becky stood in the living room doorway—a lovely sight to behold. Her dress was of the soft light blue material, which hung from the narrow belt in long straight folds. Unlike the custom of the day to wear the skirt length at the knee, Becky's dress was a little long. The rough neck and puffed sleeves innocently revealed her lovely figure. From her shoulder fell a spray of pastel satin flowers—

they were all the adornment she wore——there being not even a buckle on her blue satin slippers.

Dr. Stone didn't notice much about the dress—what held his mind was the exquisite cameo-like features above it. Becky was beautiful. Her black hair, drawn back tightly and coiled softly on the nape of her neck with only a stray little curl here and there, made a memory the likes of which few women could ever claim. When her clear blue eyes looked at Dr. Stone from beneath her gently curved black brows, he unconsciously held his breath.

"Andy dear, have you your violin music handy," she said smiling—"Tom Pendelton will want some of the old-time dances."

"I have it all in my head, Sis," he answered brightly, fitting his cherished old violin beneath his chin and drawing his bow skillfully over the strings, while he played a brilliant cadenza.

"Oh I say," breathed Dr. Stone, "but you are a regular Romeo. All the girls will be going south if you look like this often and play that way."

"You like Andy in white flannels?" said Becky happily. "So do I. He works so hard everyday, he doesn't have much time to devote to his music, but we usually play nearly an hour a day for Grandfather's sake. Andy dear, I believe someone is already here—let's go see."

It proved to be Elvira with her two sons. Lucy met her at the screen door and opened it for her.

"Bless your heart, dear," she said, "you're early, I like early folks."

"Well, seein' as I promised to make that cake I just got a move on that carried me so fast I couldn't end up here no other time. Lucy, I do think you look very gay for your days, with your lavender and lace dress on. Look at me -- I've had this little dark blue dotted-swiss for nine years now."

"I been a tellin' her to get a new one," said Charlie Hudnut, blushing red under his tan, "but she --"

"There now, Charlie, don't do no explainin' fer me. I like my dresses long and full like they use ter wear 'em. I ain't never been no hand to hike my clothes up like some I see nowadays. They say it is modern to be thet way. But I don't think so — I'll bet thet style is as old as Sodom and Gomorrahie."

Elvira raised her old head proudly and softly caressed the bit of lace that lay folded and pinned at her throat. Becky always admired this old lady immensely but couldn't help but wonder why she persisted in wearing such a marvelous gray and black wig. Tonight its waves lay in perfect order, pinned under a closely drawn net.

While the Pendeltons arrived, Elvira seated herself close to Elder Thorensen and began to ask him a lot of questions about where he had been since she had last seen him.

"I declare, Tom," whispered Cora after they were seated and Lucy was busy receiving more guests. "There is that Mormon elder again. He was here last year. I'll bet that other guy is with him too. I think the Madisons certainly have got their nerves."

"Hush, Cora, it isn't any of our affair – I reckon this here is a free country. Leastwise, the Constitution says it is."

Tom Pendelton had brought his whole family. Leander happened to be sitting on a foot-stool in front of Grandfather, exactly where he could look up – square into Elder Thorenson's face. His pinched little freckled face was turned upward in a most absorbing fashion, and his eyes, that exactly matched the color of his freckles, were taking in every change of expression in the Elder's face as he spoke.

At length a pause appeared in the conversation.

"Are you a real honest-to-goodness Mormon?" Leander asked softly, full of wonder.

"Yes my boy," Thorensen replied smilingly.

"I allus heard they had horns — I don't see yours, where are they? Mom says they've got 'em.'"

"Here Leander — this is the place for you over here!" exclaimed Cora, exasperated as she crossed the room and raised him from the stool by the coat collar. "Sit right over here by me and your pa — bring that stool along."

"I see," said Thorensen to Elvira, softly, "some folks are not out of the hills yet about our people."

"Do folks honestly say that about the Mormons?" asked Elvira incredulously.

"They certainly do and worse."

"I always did think the human race never used a tenth of their God-given sense," said Elvira indignantly, "now I know it!"

"But my dear Mrs. Hudnut," said Thorensen pleasantly, "we don't care how much they talk about us. Curiosity and uniqueness are our main aids. We are thankful we are different."

Andy came up to Dr. Stone and introduced him around the room. Everyone was glad to meet him and greeted him in a thoroughly friendly manner.

"I reckon while you are here, Doc," began Tom Pendelton, "everybody in this here neighborhood will want you to vaccinate their hogs for that dern cholera, if you're willin' to help us out. What do you say, man?"

A chorus of "Yes" arose and the doctor consented to help those who needed him. Tom Pendelton, feeling the need for some relaxation and remembering that after all this was a party, said --

"Well, now that we've gotten the work all done, let's have some music. Andy, you and George Hudnut get out them old fiddles 'o you'rn and let's get the aches out of your legs. I'm plum tired of these new fangled dances where the dancers can't get a knife blade between 'em, like Billy Sunday says; let's have some real dances, the Virginia Reel and a Quadrille."

"Tom Pendelton, you've got senses," laughed Elvira, "the young folks nowadays ain't got nothin over on we older ones. There ain't no grace and elegance about the new dances, all it consists of is a lot of foot-stamping and huggin' to an abominable rhythm."

By this time the fiddles were tuned up and playing, the furniture on the porch pushed back and also in the big living room, so that each room could hold a set. Frank Hendricks, a rather silent member of the party, proved after all to be an excellent caller.

Dr. Stone had not danced the old dances in years. Andy introduced him to Jane and Charlotte Pendelton, and he led Charlotte away in turn through the figures. There was something about this old-fashioned music that gave him great delight. It was so sociable and hospitable in spirit. He watched Becky, dancing with Tom Pendelton. She seemed perfectly at home, dancing in and out with ease, never faltering in what came next. He wished he was as apt as she was. To his surprise they began to change partners and Becky was swung around to him. He grasped her hands with a thrill and wished she would not be changed again. However, she was soon gone, for change partners they must. He saw Elder Barton take her and a chill ran through him.

"Confound it," he murmured, "that young preacher!"

Anyhow he was happy. Here was life and real gaiety, friendship and novelty. He would look back upon this evening and remember it as a perfect painting, a jeweled memory. They danced away until nearly twelve—Andy had long since carried Grandfather back upstairs. The evening became cool and lovely out under the trees. By the time he had danced all around and found Becky again, she informed him it was time to serve the refreshments, so kindly turned him over to Jane Pendelton.

"Isn't Becky a clever girl," gushed Jane at once. "I admire her very much. Let's sit out on the little front porch, it's so nice out there. This is such a dear old place and Becky fits into it charmingly, don't you think?" They seated themselves on the top step facing the grove of walnuts. "But dear me, she is such a homebody, studies a lot too. Nobody does that now in these times. I think it is mostly music and religion—by the way did you know they were Mormons?"

Doctor Stone felt a feeling of revulsion pass over him— he wished something would happen so he could decently excuse himself. This creature lacked sincerity to him and above all he did not like the careful sophistication of her. Before the refreshments were over he had tactfully refused a date she had hinted at. Jane was deeply chagrined and there seemed to be an open coolness between them.

Dr. Stone saw Andy slip away to take Charlotte home. Everyone was leaving and he found himself rather lost until they were all gone. Then he joined Lucy and Becky in the kitchen, Elder Thorensen and Barton were in there too.

"Did you have a nice time, folks?" asked Lucy.

"Oh my yes," said Thorensen.

"Folks around here think it's wicked to dance—or so I've heard the preacher warn them. I thought if we danced the old time way it would not be so bad," said Lucy.

"Dancing isn't a sin," said Thorensen, "if you dance as Brigham Young said you should."

"How is that?" asked the doctor.

"He said it this way," explained Thorensen, "those that keep their covenants and serve their God, if they wish to exercise themselves in any way, to rest their minds and tire their bodies, go and enjoy yourselves in the dance, and let God be in all your thoughts in this as in all things, and he will bless you."

"And didn't he say," said Elder Barton, "those who couldn't serve God with a pure heart in the dance, should not dance?"

"He evidently had the knack of putting things together with common sense then," said the doctor.

"Brigham Young had that attribute, my dear Doctor, in an astonishing degree. It was a God-given gift and he used it wisely to train the people."

Andy returned and after Becky had slipped through the rooms and put everything in order, they each retired for the night.

Chapter 6 Tea Roses and Tears

Andy raised his head from the pillow and looked out into the dawn. It was early but he could not sleep. He slipped out of bed and, after dressing, went to the kitchen, built a fire, then called his mother before going to the barn.

While he was doing the chores his mind fell upon the words Charlotte had whispered to him last night. "Andy, something somewhere is wrong. Watch and be careful."

He had reassured her and told her he did not feel alarmed.

"But Andy," she answered, "I know it looks foolish, but I am worried for fear there is some kind of trouble ahead."

She had been so earnest about it that, in the shadows of the night, it seemed to gather weight, but this bright sunshiny morning was something which dispelled shadows without and within.

"She works too hard in that family," he said to himself. "As soon as she decides she will have me, I'll get her out of there."

When he returned from the barn, everyone was up and the three gentlemen guests were seated on the porch reading and chatting.

"Good morning, everybody," greeted Andy jovially. "Everyone fine after the fun? Come on, let's eat, I see everything is ready."

The family breakfast was a very simple meal and was soon over. After which Dr. Stone went to the barn with Andy. Elders Thorensen and Barton remained on the porch talking to Lucy while Becky washed the dishes.

Upstairs on his pillows, peacefully resting, lay Grandfather Mahoney. He was alone but he was used to the long, long moments. They gave him opportunity to turn over in his mind the various things he found comfort in. He realized he had not long to live, but never said anything about it as it seemed so useless to do so. The thought of the party, the gay dances and the happy faces he had seen. Without regret he laid by the hope of such things in the future, as one lays aside a beautiful book. The tale of his life was told--he was like a merchant returning from a far country, with his vessel entering the quiet harbor of home. Peace and contentment rested on him as a diadem; he was waiting—longing—praying.

When Becky brought him his breakfast, she found him in a mood of silence, although he was always gentle smiling at her when their eyes met.

"Do you feel pretty good, Grandfather, after the party?"

"I feel foine, darlin', how air ye?"

"I'm happy as a duck in a brook. As soon as I get Dr. Stone's room straight and the Elders', I am going to bring you up the bowl of late roses I promised you from the garden. I am nearly done with this room now. Are you comfortable the way your pillows are?"

"Oi am jest like your duck in the brook, take my tray and thank ye. Oi am lazy, Oi belave Oi will go to sleep now."

It was so pleasant in the garden, Becky lingered as she cut the roses. She was a beautiful rose herself and having never tasted any keen penetrating sorrow her soul bore no light or marring feature about it. She bloomed as unaware of the poignancy of life as the flowers did of the frosts of winter. She knew life held grief but having never experienced it, she could not very deeply sympathize with those who had. She studied the heart of the roses.

"You tender adorable flowers," she whispered to herself, "the heart of you hidden in lovely buds, are mysteries to me. Life is so to me also. I wonder when I shall wake up and find I am really living. I marvel at the Mastermind who created all the beauties of the flowers."

Then the passage of scripture came to mind. "The eye hath not seen, the ear hath not heard, neither has it even entered into mind, the things God hath prepared for those who love him and keep his commandments."

"Oh Father," she signed as she lifted the now well-filled basket of roses, "bless all those who are in need of thy Holy Spirit with its gracious presence and let us all be thankful continually for thy many tender blessings."

Sometimes she felt lonely and rather out of the sweep of things with her companions, as if she stood apart—but always when she felt this way and asked for the presence of the Holy Spirit to be with her, a sense of sunshine filled her whole being. She seemed to know that everything was as it should be and she was at peace. Father Mahoney had early taught her this great secret of happiness. The result was that altho she was often alone, she was seldom lonely.

Becky returned to the house and went into the now tidy kitchen. She put the flowers in a lovely blue bowl and held them up.

"Isn't that a beautiful bowl of roses, Mother dear; I cut the stems quite long. I am so glad you planted all those tea roses!"

"It is very lovely, dear. Tell Father, when you take it to him, that his life has been just as sweet and tender to me as the sight and perfume of these flowers."

"That I will, Mother," Becky said, placing the bowl down on the table and tenderly took her mother's frail body in her arms.

"Oh Mother darling, it is such a lovely day—I love you—God bless you."

Freeing herself quickly, Becky picked up the bowl of flowers and carried them to her grandfather's room, leaving Lucy to wipe her eyes on the corner of her gingham apron.

"A blessing she is, and always will be to me," Lucy breathed.

Humming a bit of a song, Becky entered Grandfather Mahoney's room for the second time that morning. She put the bowl of roses on a tall pedestal near the foot of the bed.

"There, Grandfather darling, is something to feed your soul." She exclaimed joyously, "Wake up, dearie, and look."

Father Mahoney lay asleep so soundly, Becky decided not to disturb him.

"I will leave it there for him to find when he wakes up."

She turned and began to tiptoe out, glancing again at the frail form on the bed. It seemed so very quiet in the room. Not a bit of breeze stirred the curtains. She could hear distinctly the old clock ticking in the hall at the foot of the stairs. A strange sense of foreboding and the shadow of grief fell across her soul. With keen anxiety, Becky looked again at the dear face upon the pillow. He seemed asleep—but with a sharp cry she turned and ran from the room to sob out the news in her mother's arms.

It was consternation that reigned for a moment while Lucy and Becky faced the realization that what had been among them to love, was gone forever. Becky left Lucy, a saddened crushed figure, alone in the kitchen, a pan of potatoes half peeled in front of her. She rocked silently unbeknown to herself, back and forth in her straight backed clair.

"O Lord," she cried desperately, as she twisted her old apron, "I ain't going to say nothing—I can't say anything but, 'Thy will be done.'"

The tears began to come and as the flood grew less—she fell into soft deep sobs and many tears.

Swiftly, Becky ran to the barn. She found the men in the wagon shed.

"Oh Andy," she cried pitifully, "come quickly, something has happened."

Both men turned to see what was the matter. They were alarmed at the whiteness of Becky's face.

"What is it, Sis?" cried Andy, sensing her panic instantly.

"It's Grandfather!" she cried, the tears falling fast.

With a hushed breath, Andy clasped her hands and whispered--

"Dead, Becky?"

"Yes, dead."

These two children in the bloom of youth on which no breath of passing time had ever blown, locked and unlocked their hands and with stifled cries, discovered the bitterness of grief.

Douglas Stone took off his hat and stood by, his heart too full for him to speak. He came and stood close by Andy but no words would come. How well he knew what they were learning, only the expression on his face spoke for him as Andy turned to him and said --

"Come, let's go to Mother."

In the difficult time that followed, it was somehow Dr. Stone who took over the business end of the arrangements, so quietly, the household hardly realized it. Elder Thorensen and Barton proved to be of great comfort and assistance to Lucy. She was never given to much demonstration and after the first hours, she seemed to move about as in a dream. Becky telephoned to the Hudnuts and it was not long before the whole neighborhood knew—for the line between them was a party line.

Elvira came over just as the undertaker was leaving, they had brought Grandfather's body downstairs and he now lay so long, white and still beneath a sheet on a couch in the living room.

With love and tenderness in her old withered arms, Elvira reached silently for her life-long friend. Together they stood in each other's arms, Elvira's softly perfumed handkerchief did double duty and her tender hands beat a loving caress on Lucy's back.

"My dear," she said brokenly, "God is love, let all your trust be in Him."

"It is," sighed Lucy, "praise be to His holy name."

"Now all you have to do is let me manage things around here until everything is over."

"Oh, we can get along alright, Elvira, without you working so hard!"

"My gracious no, both you women look like you had been thru the flint mill—I wouldn't think 'o such a thing. Me stand around and do nothin'? Lucy, that just isn't my way."

It ended up by Elvira sending Lucy off to bed for a few hours rest while she and Becky put things to rights.

Out behind the barn Dr. Stone came upon Andy, down on his knees behind the new straw stack, where he thought he was safe from everyone. He was fervently praying—a blessing for everyone upon his lips—himself forgotten.

Dr. Stone looked at the handsome youth, so strong and steady—his fair curly hair agleam in the sun and as silently as he came, he slipped away. He profoundly wished he could pray as Andy was doing. For it was evident, Andy wasn't praying to something that was vaguely described as "a Spirit without flesh and bones, that was everywhere." This God of Andy's was undoubtedly some Being very tangible, if unseen. The doctor sighed—he had nothing but a gray sense of the unexplainable from which no comfort could be derived. Coming to the house, he became conscious of a different feeling in the household. The first acute pains over, a sense of quietude rested on the family. They seemed to accept the burden, and pick up their cross with fortitude. He saw Becky had forgotten about herself in the tender service her mother needed. The afternoon was filled by the neighbors and friends, who came bringing delicacies for the family's comfort.

Dr. Stone did not see Andy for quite a while. He saw Elders Thorensen and Barton out at the barn talking to him. It seemed rather a private conversation so he did not intrude.

That night, when the last of the company was gone, they were all gathered on the living-room porch for a bit of rest.

"Elder Thorensen, I wish you would tell us all just what you told me this afternoon," said Andy seriously. "Somehow it seems too sacred for me to tell and I would rather you would do it."

"I will repeat it, if you desire," said Elder Thorensen, "but it is a very precious experience and not to be taken lightly or doubted by anyone, as it really happened."

"That is the beautiful and comforting part. I want everyone here to hear it, for it will strengthen our faith," said Andy fervently, leaning back in his chair to listen. His eyes fell on his mother and sister and he smiled.

"It was like this," began the Elder meditatively.

"About three nights ago, I lay in a room in a hotel in Elkhart. Elder Barton was not with me then and I slept alone. I was quite weary and somewhat discouraged. I felt I was not making any headway whatsoever in this part of the state. In such a state of mind, I knelt down and in humble prayer besought the Lord to please bless my labors and give me what bit of comfort He saw fit. In a resigned frame of mind, I went to bed and lay quite still for several moments. All at once there was a queer sensation that took hold of me—something seemed to be opened somewhere for I became instantly out of the body. I saw my body lying on the bed and I realized I was dead. You may well imagine the extreme joy I experienced to find that there was no more to death than the quick passage of the spirit, and that I was alive forevermore. A guide, I had not hitherto seen, stepped from behind me and said pleasantly–

"Come go with me—

"I immediately did as he said and soon we were going up and up and up until we came to a great wall through which was a small door. This door opened wide and we went in.

"I soon realized I was in Paradise for I saw many people coming and going, along the beautiful walks, in the wonderful parks, and into the glorious buildings. There was the most exhilarating feeling of security and peace there. I was thrilled beyond measure to realize I was indeed safe 'on the Beautiful Shore'.

"The landscape was so different there, we have no language here to describe it. Instead of just green, as we have it in summer, every flower, shrub, and tree was changed into something so heavenly in color—it is as I said, we have no words to picture it.

"My guide and I walked along past many beautiful homes, where children romped on grass with flowers growing in it that were never crushed by their footsteps. We passed a beautiful clear river. People were wading in and out like children playing. Some of them crossed the stream to the wonderful flower gardens on the other side, others sat down in the clear depths of the water and chatted together. Everyone who came out seemed just as dry as they did when they went in. I asked my guide what this river was and he said it was the River of Life that flowed from beneath the Great Throne and that all who bathed in it gradually washed away every bit of their old world life, they became more susceptible to the Heavenly influences. By this time I was meeting a few of the many spirits I passed, that I had long known on earth. I was greeted with friendly nods and merry laughter. It was not long until I came upon my dear mother and father. No one can explain how happy I felt to meet them again and to have them bring others of my family I had lost to greet and welcome me. I found out a great deal about my genealogy and how to trace it through the records in the old country.

"I turned to follow my guide, when I saw approaching me along the walk I was on, a small company of people. Their white robes seemed to be the most beautiful of anything I had yet seen and in the midst of them walked a personage so benign and gracious in form, feature and manner I was at once spellbound with the realization I was face-to-face with my Lord and Savior. I was thrilled with unspeakable joy; and I fell at His feet and could only worship Him. As I did so my eyes rested on the wounds once made in His feet and I wept tears of gratitude to think they were made for me.

"With great tenderness and love He bade me arise. I did so and stood before Him enthralled at once with the great beauty of His ways and face. I perceived that He was a very familiar person to me—one I had dearly loved and had somehow missed a long while. He told me to be of good cheer about my work—that my prayers were heard and before long I would bring into His church some precious souls. He then passed on in the glorious company of saints and I was left alone with my smiling guide.

"'Isn't it wonderful to think He would stop to greet me?' I said slowly, gazing after His commanding figure.

"'That is the way of the Christ,' returned my guide, as happy as I was. 'He always greets everyone in their turn and feeds them with the Living Bread. I think it is about time we returned now.'

"I did not want to go back—but he informed me I had a great work to do yet and that I must go. We turned and began to take another path through the parks. At last we came to the building close to the small door where I had come in. Passing by an open window, I saw Mrs. Pearson an old neighbor of mine in Salt Lake. She was delighted to see me and urged me to come in a moment.

We did so and found a roomful of women sewing on beautiful white robes, the like of which they themselves wore. We talked of old times and she inquired about her family on earth. I told her all the news I could think of and was just about to go when I asked her who the robes were for that she and her friends were making. She named over a few friends in the West I have not seen for years and lastly spoke of Father Mahoney.

"'This one I am working on is for him—we expect him day after tomorrow.'

"My guide now urged me to return and we bade them goodbye and I went through the little door I had come in at. Immediately I felt myself going through gray space and presently I was back in my body in that lonely hotel room. The pain I felt at leaving the body was nothing to what I experienced on re-entering it. I was so awestruck and filled with so much amazement I never slept much that night. On waking in the morning, I made up my mind to come to you here as I felt you would need me. From what Father Mahoney told me last year when I was here, He wanted me to be here at a time like this. So I came, having met Elder Barton the next day. I brought him along also."

"What a wonderful experience," said Becky reverently. "It is so much comfort, Mother darling, let us be of good cheer—he is not dead but gone into that larger life."

"I believe you are right there, dear," said Lucy warmly, "it would not be pleasing in God's sight to grieve too deeply. We should trust Him fully."

"My gracious," exclaimed Elvira, "that takes my breath plum away. I ain't never heared sech comfortin' words in all my life. I think these must, fer a fact, be the last days. My old Bible tells me that when thet time comes the young men shall dream dreams and the old men see visions."

"You are right, Elvira," said Lucy, "it is the fulfillment of prophecy, and according to the Bible too, but the unbelieving world scoffs at such a thing."

"And you really saw that vision, Elder Thorensen? I can't hardly believe it yet," queried Elvira, filled with wonder still.

"I really did, Mrs. Hudnut, and let me assure you no mortal ever hated to leave any place as badly as I did that Heavenly Home. We mortals miss a lot of happiness by not taking Christ at his simple words in the old Book— we do entirely too much spiritualizing."

"I wish, Andy, you would give me some of your books to read," said Elvira with determination. "I don't care what folks will say about Elvira Hudnut, I'm sick of most of 'em anyhow. They're jest like dry clouds sailing over me. There ain't been nobody fer years let any rain out on my soul, like whut 'o you'rn contain what I think they will, I'm going West with you Madisons and there isn't nothin' goin' ter stop me."

"I will give you a Book of Mormon with the greatest of pleasure, Sister Hudnut," said Elder Thorensen, "and furthermore, I will tell you that you are of the pure blood of Ephriam, that you will love this Gospel with all your heart and cleave unto it for the rest of your days."

"Well, I'll be--," said Elvira, her withered face working and the tears running down through the wrinkles. "I wish I wuz forty years younger."

"You have your genealogy, haven't you, away back?"

"You mean my family-tree?"

"Yes."

"Land sakes, I got a family-tree over there to the house, that covers the whole dining table. I ain't niver been much of a hand at sech things but my husband wuz. And when he wuz alive he wuz allus writin' from Maine ter Jericho ter find out every living member uv the whole Hudnut family. I use ter tell him he might jest as well take the Hud offen his name, he didn't need it any longer—Mr. Nut would do jest as well, he acted just like one over sech things."

"And you always kept it?" questioned both elders at once.

"Well, I wuz goin' ter burn it up, but after he wuz gone the boys tuck a fancy to it and said I'd better keep it. I told 'em they wasn't doin' the pesky thing no good—thet they ought ter git married and put some more names under theirn and their wives. But thet's all the good hit done. George says he ain't got a chance with the woman he wants, but try as I do, I can't find out who she is."

There were so many people coming and going the next day and evening, the family were quite worn out by the day of the funeral. It was with a great sense of relief that Dr. Stone saw the last of the friends depart. Elvira and Charlotte did not go to the services at the little stone church. They stayed at home and prepared supper for the family.

At the church there was no standing room. Father Mahoney had lived many years in the neighborhood and was greatly beloved and respected, if considered rather queer in his religion. Everyone listened attentively to the words of the Mormon elder. Many considered it the best funeral sermon they had ever listened to, because he spoke with such calm assurance of the Resurrection and

107

of the life lived in the Spirit World. Elder Barton dedicated the grave. There were many whose eyes were wet. The beauty of this custom practiced among Latter-Day Saints impressed them greatly.

It was quite dusk when Elvira and Charlotte said they must go. Andy went with Charlotte down the long twilight-shadowed road. They passed George Hudnut at the lane-gate, coming in his car after his mother.

"Your mother is sound asleep, Becky, don't awaken her. I'm takin' these elders home with me, as I want to keep them a few days."

"Sit down, all of you, just a minute before we go, I have some little books as tokens of remembrance to leave with you," said Elder Thorensen, rising from his chair and going into the house. Presently he was back.

"I have this little book to leave with each household or friend here. It is a great little book and I am sure you will all enjoy it. I love what it says so much, I am always buying it and scattering the words among my friends."

He quickly gave one to Elvira, Becky and Dr. Stone.

"With my compliments, folks, and may you long enjoy the words written therein. Shall we go now, Sister Hudnut?"

Becky bid her old friend goodbye and she and Dr. Stone sat alone on the front porch. They both opened the little blue bound books that Thorensen had given them. It was entitled "Added Upon" and was written by Nephi Andersen.

"What an odd title," thought Dr. Stone, "wonder what it means?"

When Andy returned, Dr. Stone and Becky were half through their books. They were sitting by the lighted lamp in the spacious old sitting-room, as excited as could be. The elders were gone and the house was quiet as before.

Upstairs in his room, Dr. Stone lay reading long after they had all retired for the night.

"If I don't watch out," he said earnestly, as he put out the light, "that little book is going to change my whole life."

Chapter 7 Cholera

Next morning Dr. Stone was awakened by Andy's knock at the door. He arose and dressed quickly. When he got downstairs, Becky was setting the table. Becky and Lucy said at breakfast they should go to Riversdale on business that morning. So after the work was done, Becky drove away with her mother. Andy and Dr. Stone began the work of inoculating the hogs for cholera.

It was a hot dusty day. The hogs were milling around in the barn lot. Andy drove them in the barn door one at a time, and then they gave them a shot of serum. They counted each one to make sure they had not left any in the woods.

At last Andy drove a big black one into the barn. It seemed to be alright just to glance at it—but Dr. Stone knew better the minute his eyes fell on it.

"If that isn't a hog with the cholera, Andy, I'll eat my doctor's license," he said seriously.

"Pon my word, come to look at it good—it isn't my hog either," said Andy.

"Whose is it then?"

"I'm sure I don't know."

"If I was you, I'd never give it any serum—take it out, shoot and burn it."

Andy lost no time in doing what he was told and burnt it on a brush pile in the old orchard.

By the time Andy got back, the doctor had inoculated several more. He was not surprised to run across two who already had the cholera. Before the morning's work was done they found that over half the hogs were reactors to the serum and the work had to be done again. Andy was pretty blue.

When Lucy and Becky returned, they quickly took the dinner from the fireless cooker and set the table as usual on the porch. Lucy noticed the sad expression on Andy's face but said nothing until the meal was nearly done.

"How are the hogs, Andy dear?" she asked gently.

"Not so good, Mother."

"Have they got the cholera?"

"Yes, Mother, over half of them."

"But Dr. Stone, how could they have gotten it—Andy has been so careful?"

"I don't know, Mrs. Madison. There was a strange hog in the bunch that was sick with it."

"Oh Andy, you don't suppose, do you?" Becky stopped short and gazed strongly at Andy, while inwardly she saw things as they were. The remembrance of Charlotte's warning flew into Andy's mind.

"Well, it could be, Sis—but that certainly is a low, underhanded trick!"

At the barn, Dr. Stone asked if he might know what it was all about. With a gesture of exasperation at the way matters were turning out, Andy unfolded the whole miserable story of Ezra Weeks. Then how because of the fall in farm prices since the war, they had been forced to mortgage the place. It was an old story but nevertheless a true one, and to hear it this time made Douglas Stone's heart ache. It gradually unfolded that John Manning held the mortgage.

"If I know anything about John Manning, he will not hold back one second to take the place from us. It would do him good—now that Becky has refused to marry his son, Cicil, he would like nothing better than to make us homeless." Andy's voice was full of bitterness and he flung the words out viciously.

"Oh I see, " said Dr. Stone, "this Manning, is he the jaybird that they say has the big boot-leg ring? I've heard it goes all over the northern part of the state."

"Yes, he's the grand mogul of Riversdale. He does as he pleases any place. It made him very much put out when Becky turned his boy down. I reckon he thought she would just jump at the chance to be in the Manning family. He has been treating us queer ever since. If he finds out my hogs are sick, he will know I can't raise the mortgage money and it won't be a week before he will be out here on Mother to worry her to death."

"When is the mortgage due?"

"The twentieth—this is the fifteenth, so I guess I'm sunk alright—alright!"

Andy picked up a shovel and went to the crib to get corn to feed the hogs that would eat.

Dr. Stone, left by himself, picked up his watch fob and began to turn it from side to side slowly and rather absently. He was thinking deeply.

Evening came and Andy seemed to recede more and more to himself. Lucy sat nearby in the sitting room doing a bit of mending. She finally folded her hands and looked out upon the quiet scene about her. It had been a hard week. She was weary. But the mercy of God unfolded to her the wisdom of the turn in her life's path. As of old she questioned not. She realized she was on the verge of losing all that she held dear, her home and everything, but she said--

"Father, you will please have to take the burden into your hands and do as it is best. I can no longer worry with such conditions."

Someday before long, she knew they must go West and do the Temple work. Why should it be put off any longer, she reasoned.

In the soft twilight Andy and Dr. Stone sat on the front porch and rested. The peace and quiet of the scene fell upon them like a mantle of bliss. The grove of trees was enchanting in the soft shadows of night—as the crickets chirped pleasantly in the grass. All the world seemed at peace.

Becky had gone into the parlor and opened the piano. It was the first piano music Dr. Stone had heard in the Madison home and the room she sat in he had never entered.

Anyone could tell the music she played was unwritten—as her fingers strayed from one cadenza to another with a freedom and abandon that was without previous meditation. Gradually among the changing chords and arpeggios, the theme of an old love song crept in. The beautiful words came into the minds of the listeners and they were thrilled by the charm of them.

"Once in the dear dead days beyond recall,
When on the earth the mist began to fall,
Out of the dreams that rose in happy throng,
So to our hearts, love sang an old sweet song."

Memories of a big brick house, with white massive pillars and a little boy playing on the wide porch steps, crossed Dr. Stone's mind. The perfume of French violets mingled once more with that of white lilacs. Dr. Stone was carried back to bye-gone days and became a child in spirit. Within the house, he saw his mother once again, seated at the old-fashioned square piano. She wore an elegant gown, long, white and very full in the skirt. There were dainty sprays of lavender flowers cast over it in a delicate pattern, mingled with shaded green leaves. By her side stood his father—tall and darkly handsome in a dress suit. They were both very beautiful to him now that he could look back upon them in the enchanting way that childhood's vision framed tender memories. She had played gently the same strain Becky's fingers were now harmonizing, and they had lifted their voices and sang together in a beautiful soprano and tender tenor. It was so exquisite a picture the little boy never forgot it and now that he was a man it came back to him as beautiful as ever. It was the last memory he had of his father; the shadow fell across his mother's life soon after and it was not long before he was left to mourn them both.

"It is too soon to speak, Andy, but I think I had better go away in a few days. I must tend to these hogs of Pendelton's—then I think I will go. Shall I ever come back? I want her for my wife, I love her very much."

Andy was surprised and yet he wasn't.

"I am sure that is up to you and Becky," he said gently, "she has said she will never marry outside of our church—as you are not a member—I think you ought to know that much."

"That's just it, Andy, I've never been interested in religion before but I am taken up with the idea of investigating this religion of yours."

"I am very glad to hear it," said Andy.

"If I do, I think it no more than fair that I do all that deciding before I ask her. I don't want her to think I am accepting her religion just to get her for my wife. So Andy, I think I had better go and begin my studies of your faith. It is going to be a struggle as I have almost become an unbeliever in anything but I'll make the effort. I am going to Michigan and you may not hear anything from me for quite awhile--but Andy, try to keep me in mind before her, for I hope to come back. Will you" Dr. Stone faltered.

"We may not be in this country very much longer—then you would not find us if you came here," said Andy.

"I will inquire and if you are not in Indiana any longer, I will go to Salt Lake City and trust I can find you there. I'll be able to find you, don't worry about that. It may take a year or more to do what I am going to do."

Becky appeared at the front door.

"Oh Andy," she said happily, "come get your violin, it has been over a week since we've played together."

"I will, Sis, if you'll play the gypsy music."

"Don't you think we had better not be so gay yet awhile?"

"No, I don't think it out of the way. I know Grandfather would want us all to be happy," said Andy.

The two men came into the parlor—it was really the music room. The walls were white and paneled in a very simple molding. The ceiling was high as in all the rooms. There was a spacious fireplace, as in the living room, for the old house was graced with huge chimneys at each end. The floor was highly polished and waxed all over— here and there hooked rugs were scattered over it. Few pictures graced the walls but those that were there, were excellent copies of some of Sir Joshua Reynold's portraits. Over in the corner of the room away from the windows stood the only modern thing in the house—a beautiful baby-grand piano. An elegant Persian scarf with heavy fringe lay across its polished surface on which sat a low round antique bowl full of delicate shades of blue delphinium, baby's breath and coral-shaded aster. The sight of these flowers in combination with the dull yellow bowl brought exclamations of pleasure from the two men.

"Gee, Sis, that is a creation you have there," said Andy happily.

"It is indeed, you are an artist, Miss Becky."

"I like the simple old-fashioned flowers, Doctor. I get more thrill out of a flower catalog than a movie."

"Sit down, Doctor, anywhere and we will try to play for you." Andy drew the cherished violin from its old case and began to tune up as Becky, already seated at the piano, gave him the notes. "What shall we play first, do you like the old tunes?"

"I certainly do," responded the doctor quickly, "do you play the 'Last Rose of Summer'?"

"Listen," said Andy.

Doctor Stone, seated in a low Windsor rocker by the open window, looked out into the moonlit grove. A gentle breeze fanned the dainty lace curtains that were gracefully draped back on either side. The soft strains of music blended into the twilight and Dr. Stone realized Father Time was painting another memory.

The gentle pathos of the old melody fitted consolingly into the halls of his heart, soothing the sorrows of the past gently away, healing like beautiful vines covering the scars of the forest. He became more reconciled to the baffling problems of existence and sweet peace like a stream, watering thirsty ground, flooded his soul. Dr. Stone felt as the last notes of the exquisite harmony from the two instruments died away, that Life after all was like walking in a beautiful garden, created by a supernatural power which was capable of meeting every emergency effectively.

The players ceased a moment and Andy leaned over and spoke to his sister in a low tone. Presently the inexpressible sweetness of the heavenly strains composed by Saint Saens came throbbing through their beloved instruments. It was the vision of "The Swan."

Dr. Stone had been in many cities of the world and heard various celebrated artists—but it gave him more enjoyment to sit in this quiet country house, with its atmosphere of bygone days, and listen to these two musicians than all the rest he had ever heard. They evidently had the vision of things, and had worked unceasingly to attain the ease and finished poise with which they were endowed. He knew they had been born with the one vital spark of genius and that they were capable of taking all the education that could be put upon them.

He watched the naturalness of Becky and was charmed with her more than ever. Sitting there in her simple cotton voile dress, her figure was alive with youth and beauty but he realized the soul within was one he could love forever—no matter what the storms of the years might do. If he was in love with Becky when he first sat down, now to that love was added the fire of infatuation.

From Schubert's "Ave Maria" they turned lightly to his "Moment Musical." It was saturated with a blithesome rhythm which paved the way naturally to the bewitching Hungarian Dances of Brahms and Liszt. This music was the spice of life to the musicians. They cast all restrictions aside and let their imaginations roam. The music flowed as easily and gracefully as a silken scarf floats in the wind.

"Oh, I say," breathed Dr. Stone, fascinated, "but do you two know how well you really do play?"

Becky turned around on the piano bench, gripped her slender fingers nervously—while Andy wiped the perspiration from his face with his handkerchief.

"Do you really enjoy it too?" She asked breathlessly. Dr. Stone saw at once she had not had him in mind while she was playing at all.

"Do I?" his voice was full of admiration. "Why, it's great!"

In his mind's eye he saw them both studying in the famous schools of France and eventually winning the renown they, by the gift of Nature, deserved.

Andy laid down the violin carefully and sought a chair. "That is enough for one night," he said.

"Who taught you both to play?"

"We have a teacher in town who is quite a master—but we haven't taken for quite a while," explained Andy. "Sis likes to play and so do I and we keep pegging away at it everyday steady."

"That's the secret of it—you have worked and worked hard."

"There is no royal road to learning," laughed Becky, "and the music muse is especially hard to please."

Becky arose and left the room, saying she would be back presently. In a little while she returned—a tall glass of red punch on each plate, beside two large slices of angel food cake. She gave each a linen napkin and said to Doctor Stone, as she gave him his plate--

"This is Andy's weakness!"

"I know mine when I see it too," replied the doctor gallantly, winking mischievously at Andy.

Chapter 8 Becky's a Peach

When morning came and breakfast passed, Dr. Stone said he thought it best to go over to the Pendeltons and work that day. It did not take long for him to drive down the road to their house. He turned into the driveway just as Tom Pendelton was coming to the house with the morning's milk.

"Hello there," Tom greeted him wholeheartedly. "Ready for work?"

"If you are," said the doctor getting out of the car.

"I'll be out in a jiffy, got to take the milk in and separate it," Pendelton disappeared into the house.

Cora met him as he came in. "Is that man going to be here for dinner, Tom?" she asked vexed.

"Yes sirree, he is."

"What?"

"That's what I said, and put on the high style, too, will ya, Ma?"

Unmindful of the taken-aback expression on Cora's face, Tom studiously poured the milk in the huge bowl of the separator, through the strainer cloth she silently adjusted, and commenced turning the crank. There was an air of finality about the way he dictated his order, that left her powerless to contradict him, but it didn't check her rising resentment. He silently laid down the handle to the machine and picked up the pails of skimmed milk. Without a look, he went out the kitchen door to the barn. Speechless, she took the cream can to the cellar, vigorously shaking her head.

Aunt Em came into the kitchen from feeding the chickens just as Cora emerged from the cellar doorway.

"Lands sakes, Corie, but this is going to be another hot day—I never seen the beat, I'm jes plum tuckered out, and it ain't eight o'clock yet!" Aunt Em swung her blue sun-bonnet back and forth to fan herself as she dropped exhausted in a chair.

"That's nothin'!" snorted Cora.

"What's up now?" demanded Em emphatically.

"Oh nothin', only Tom says company dinner today for that hog doctor. I don't see why it had to be today. I had just planned on a little snack, so I could go to the Ladies Aid Society–Sara Thatcher said everybody was to be sure and be there. This weather is a fright–jest terrible on my high blood-pressure–and eating' is jest about as high as a man ever gets. He never thinks about how hard it is on the woman!"

Aunt Em knew well enough when to sit silent. Cora's temper was like the wind–it just naturally blew itself out. She heaved a sigh but Cora didn't hear it. Cora was talking about not being able to use paper plates and paper tablecloth.

Cora was getting hotter and hotter when, all unthought of, Jane came into the kitchen. Her hair wasn't combed, she wore a faded blue kimono and run-down slippers that clicked lazily at every step.

"What's all the row?" she yawned.

"Ah nothin'," said Aunt Em mildly, evidently trying to pour oil on the troubled waters. "Your pa has just insisted we do this cow-and-hog doctor up brown like Lucy Madison has been doing–and Cora thinks she has enough to do."

"Well, I've never seen the day yet, when a Madison laid a Pendelton in the shade! What's the matter, Ma, of course we are going to give him a swell dinner, and one tonight, too."

Jane spoke without looking at either of the women, yawned lazily again, gently tapping her fingers over her mouth, and left the room, saying–

"I'll send Charlotte right down to help with the work. Don't worry, everything will be grand."

Cora never looked at Em–nor Em at Cora, but both set to work.

Out at the barn, Dr. Stone had his business started and was casually trying to make the acquaintance of Ezra Weeks. Ezra didn't have much of anything to say. He was busy chewing tobacco. He was at hand to do what Tom told him to do–but in the meantime he lolled indolently against the hayloft ladder and indulged in the pleasant art of sending a stream of liquid tobacco clear across the driveway in the barn now and then. His red hair, extremely thin face and watery blue eyes, narrowed down usually until they were mere slits in his face, presented an appearance of utter neglect and unmanliness that nauseated Dr. Stone.

As the doctor tried time and again, unsuccessfully, to draw Ezra into a conversation, he eventually came to the conclusion that the man was too dull and stupid to carry on any conversation intelligently.

"How'd Andy's hogs come out?" queried Tom.

"Not very good, Mr. Pendelton," replied Dr. Stone, with a watchful eye on Ezra. "They have the cholera pretty bad and I will be surprised if he has twenty five left out of the hundred and thirty."

"Shucks, it ain't that bad, is it?" said Tom sadly. "I like that boy and if he loses them hogs–it will just make him lose out all around."

"Funny thing where that hog came from," said the doctor easily.

"What d' you mean?"

"Well, I don't know where it ever came from, neither does Andy, but there was the sickest hog over there you ever saw. It was a big black one with one white foot. Did you ever see a hog like that around here in the neighborhood?"

"Not as I know of," said Tom, scratching his head with his hat in his hand. "Me and Ez here had one apiece like that last spring–but we figured on killin' 'em. I did mine and supposed he did his."

Dr. Stone, out of the corner of his eye, saw Ezra ease away to the other side of the barn and begin to busy himself, cleaning the horse stalls. The atmosphere was charged with unexplained feelings. Dr. Stone thought he understood.

"Well, I'll swan," said Tom meekly and wide-eyed. "That is the first time in a year, I ever saw that guy go to work without me tellin' him!"

In the house upstairs, Charlotte had been wrestling out her serious problem since the wee small hours of the morning. She knew that the Gospel in the books Andy had given her was true. The Book of Mormon which Becky had given her the night of the party, filled her with a great deal of happiness. But there was the question of whether she would follow where it led her or not.

She had awakened extremely early and slipped out of bed. Sitting in her easy chair by her open windows, she had read and reread through the thrilling chapters of the old Nephite prophet, Nephi. Earnestly she knelt by her chair and asked her Heavenly Father if he would not witness unto her by the power of the Holy Spirit, that the words of the book were true. Immediately a flood of warmth and joy passed over her that burned intently into her heart.

When she arose from her knees, she was filled with an ardent desire to be baptized and embrace this gospel. She knew that she loved Andy—but here was a love which transcended everything she had ever known. She felt a desire to turn others to her faith and was blessed with a sense of peace and happiness she had never known before.

She was awakened from her reveries on the subject by someone at her door. She barely had enough time to hide her precious books under the rug and beneath her mattress when the door was rudely flung open. There stood Jane, indolently eyeing her.

"What are you doing, up here all by yourself this late in the morning, with your door shut? Don't you know it's late and going to be hotter than blazes?"

Charlotte said nothing. Here was a bit of real life to be lived out in practice—not in theory as the books have it.

"I was resting, and I like to be alone sometimes, Jane. Everybody does."

"We're not going to be alone today, I can tell you. You had better get a move on—and go down and help Ma while I dress. She is madder than a—"

Jane's orders were interrupted by the stair door opening and Leander came bouncing up the stairs in muddy overalls.

"Leander Pendelton!" snapped Jane, "the nerve of you—the idea of a boy coming upstairs in such a mess. Where have you been?"

"I've been out to the barn helping Pa, the same as you ought ter be downstairs helping Ma!"

"I'll teach you something, young man!" Jane made a wild dash after Leander, but that young scalawag darted past her into the open door of Jane's room. The door shut with a bang—locking it.

"Help me, Charlotte, he will ruin everything I got," cried Jane, pounding on her door with her little fists until her extremely long polished nails pressed deep into the flesh. "Let me in!" she almost screamed.

"Since when," began Charlotte evenly, "have you ever had the authority to correct that child. That isn't your place and now that you have trouble on your hands you want me to pull you out. Leander, open the door, I won't let her hurt you! There, that's a good boy."

The bedroom door swung open slowly. The girls just caught a glimpse of a pair of dirty overall legs in the act of dragging themselves over a pink silk bedspread and disappearing through an open front window.

"That darn little wretch!" exclaimed Jane, making another dash toward the window—but the fleeing little freckle-faced urchin was gone. She turned in fury on Charlotte like an angry leopard.

"You're the cause of all this, Charlotte Pendelton," she blazed, "and you can just clean up this room for it."

"I don't think I will do any such a thing this time, Jane," said Charlotte firmly. "You haven't straightened up your room for a week. I'm tired of being your slave and it can lay as it is. You have the lazy fashion of dropping your clothes any old place and never picking them up. It's time you learned to work, young lady!"

Without a backward glance, Charlotte turned and ran lightly down the stairs, leaving Jane staring after her speechless in amazement.

"The little hussy!" said Jane, perfectly white in the face. "I'll fix her!"

In a rage, Jane flounced into her own room and slammed the door shut. She paid no attention to the general view of her wrecked room but hastily and without thought began to sling things out of her sight into the closet. Her anger made her almost blind and the steel blue of her eyes glittered dangerously.

"If what I think about her is correct, I'll soon fix her. She won't have even a look in!"

Downstairs unmindful of the gathering storm, Charlotte sang softly to herself. She brushed up what rooms needed it–dusted and arranged some flowers from the long rows in the vegetable garden.

Aunt Em opened the kitchen door and came into the dining room with wide eyes and surprise in her face. Charlotte had the table set for company. The nice linen and silver were out and to cap it all off, a beautiful centerpiece of pansies and fern sat in the center of the long table.

"Did Jane tell you to do all this?" Aunt Em asked gently.

"Land no, I'm done taking orders from that larky. I am afraid if she wants anything done in the future–she must do it herself. I'm nineteen years old and I'm not going to be little sister any more."

"Good for you, I hope you get away with it," smiled Aunt Em putting her tender old arms around Charlotte. "Shall I bake a sponge cake for you? I'll light the oil stove out on the back porch."

"That will be lovely, Auntie," said Charlotte. "I'm not trying to vamp the doctor, you understand, honey–but it won't hurt her if she thinks I am. She can't stand to see Becky have a friend, so she has to try her wiles on him. I'm getting tired of it."

"You do like the Madisons, don't you?" said Aunt Em.

"Certainly. They are nice to me and I like to go there."

"Well honey, don't think too much—take that bit of advice from old Aunt Em. It just won't ever do."

Aunt Em went to the kitchen and started the sponge cake—. Charlotte went upstairs and put on a clean print dress. She came into the kitchen just as her father and Dr. Stone were coming into the house. Cora's face was rather hard and she did not even try to be friendly to the guest. Charlotte saw how matters were and tried to make things as pleasant as possible by bringing fresh towels and afterward she took her father and the doctor into the living room until lunch was ready.

At no time had Charlotte seen Jane since her encounter with her. She went ahead putting the chairs to the table and doing the duties that fell to her lot in a peaceful frame of mind. When everything was ready she called everyone to the meal and quietly seated herself along with the rest of the family. Jane's footsteps were heard on the stairs, and every eye was turned toward her as she entered. She was fresh and cool in a demure frock that

Charlotte knew must have cost thrice what her father could afford. As the blessing was asked the last of it was interrupted by the telephone ringing. Charlotte arose and answered it. The call was for Ezra. She told him so and set the phone down for him. As she was seating herself at the table, it came to her with a start who the speaker was at the other end of the line. Her heart was pounding furiously as she heard Ezra say—

"yes, tonight,"

As much like the sphinx as ever, Ezra took his place again at the table.

Jane Pendelton knew she was good looking; so with the confidence that comes from such assurance, she began to sparkle vivaciously. But for once with a steady spirit underneath her control, Charlotte deftly turned the conversation on to the subject of travel, skillfully drawing the doctor out to tell of his many wonderful experiences in the Army of Occupation overseas. Jane was like a spoiled child. She sat taking no part in the conversation, looking puzzled at times, to her mother for consolation.

The luncheon was soon finished. As the men returned eagerly to work, Charlotte did likewise. She helped Aunt Em, singing blithely all the time and entirely ignoring the coolness with which Jane treated her. Jane silently returned to her room. Cora got ready and went to the Ladies Aid Society.

"Go lay down and get your rest, Auntie. I'd rather you would, it's too hot for you in this kitchen," said Charlotte. "I'll pick things up and then wash the dishes."

Aunt Em gladly went, for she suffered from asthma and hay fever, and she was soon snoring gently on the living room couch.

Charlotte, left all alone, busied herself with putting things in order. After a brief rest she dressed two frying chickens, made a vegetable salad, and two cherry pies. These she put away to cool on the shelves down in the cellar, then prepared the potatoes and beans to cook for supper. Contented and happy, she went to her room and, after bathing, dressed herself in the gay flowered voile dress that she knew Andy especially liked.

When Tom Pendelton came in with Dr. Stone and Ezra, he found the house cool, the meal ready, and a happy Charlotte to greet him. Cora came home just in time to set herself down to supper.

"I think you are lucky, Pendelton," said Dr. Stone, "to have no reactors in your bunch. The cholera seems to be bad around here."

"I'm thankful as can be," said Tom. "Have some more chicken, doctor, that's one good thing 'o living' on the farm. The farmers have got it in the neck lots of ways— but they ain't lost their chicken yet, by George." Tom Pendelton laughed happily.

Douglas Stone looked at Ezra. He was washed until his skin shone a shining pink and white where his hat had shaded his face. The rest of his face, hands and arms were sunburnt a dark reddish brown. It was a silent Ezra, with down-cast eyes, too busy to prove himself sociable, who sat there literally forking the food into his mouth in huge helpings.

The cherry pie was received with a hearty welcome by Tom.

"Here is the pie of all pies, doctor. Have a piece," said Tom proudly. "Charlotte knows how to make everything, the fellar that gits her will be apt to be darn glad of it 'fore he gits done."

Cora and Jane exchanged glances, while Aunt Em, who was hugely enjoying the meal, didn't help by adding knowingly-

"I'll say he will, Tom, I've seen to that. Charlotte's a good cook!"

So it was that the big surprise came to Charlotte, the chance she had been praying for–to see Andy.

"Your father is exactly right, Miss Charlotte," said Dr. Stone, a merry twinkle dancing in his eye. "I am going up the road a little ways pretty soon–won't you please come along?"

"Pon my word!" roared Tom Pendelton. "You sure know a good thing when you see it–Miss Becky is a peach!"

Dr. Stone blushed slightly but replied easily–

"Far be it from me, Pendelton, to be blind to what I see. Will you go with me, Miss Charlotte," asked the doctor again, through the hilarity.

"I might as well," she blushed, "it is going to be a lovely evening."

When they arose from the table, Charlotte started to help Aunt Em with the dishes, but just then Tom took his knife and plate out of her hands and said firmly–

"Just run along and get ready, young lady. Jane here will help with the dishes, you have worked all day!"

Jane gave a little gasp at the way things were turning out. In an ugly mood she turned and went quickly into the kitchen, followed by Cora.

Three-quarters of an hour later, it was a very bitter Jane who stood at her upstairs window, and watched Charlotte stroll off with the man she had hoped so ardently to entice. Cecil Manning was forgotten. Here was a real man; a man who would always command a good position, and she was as powerless to attract him as vinegar to entice bees. Living for admiration only, everything was dust and ashes when she failed to receive it. A well of bitterness and fury surged up within her and, turning fiercely on her high heels, she darted swiftly into Charlotte's room and slammed the door shut behind her.

Chapter 9 A river like a sunken mirror

Dr. Stone, walking beside Charlotte down the narrow shaded river road, was charmed by the quiet beauty of the scene about him, that lay bathed so gently in the soft August twilight. It awakened old songs and old memories. He knew that these days he had been living would be stamped forever upon his memory, in colors as fresh and varied as their living image.

The slowly meandering river, with the flickering reflection of giant trees upon its wide expanse, the tender green of slender rushes growing close upon its bosom, the sparkling sheen of lights playing far out in midstream, and the mellow harmony of its ever-flowing gentleness, were all realities that would remain forever living pictures in the gallery of pleasant memories.

They came around a gentle curve in the sandy auto-tracked road, which opened up to view a massed bed of rich purple asters intermingled with the waving plumes of gorgeous golden-rod, standing in their wild graceful abandon against a hedge of satin leaved bittersweet.

"It is so very beautiful through here," commented the doctor.

"I think so too," said Charlotte proudly, "I often wonder if the first great garden was any more beautiful than this, my native soil. I often think too, this ought to be the setting of some charming book, but I am too numb in speech to paint it."

"So it ought," Dr. Stone mused admiringly. "Gene Stratton Porter should have written a tale about the Wabash."

"Yes, but then that romantic old song has caught the charm and appeal of these shaded woodlands wonderfully well."

"Thru the sycamores the candle
   lights are gleaming,
On the banks of the Wabash,
   far away."

Charlotte sang lightly. "I wonder, Dr. Stone, if either you or I will eventually wander far away from this old state to find a home and live and die there?"

"This is food for the soul, but I am afraid I have the wanderlust. I think if one spot on this globe can be so attractive, what can the rest be like?"

"So it is," sighed Charlotte, "and little birds have a way of flying out of the nest."

"Nor will the time be long, Miss Charlotte, before you will be flying if all the signs are correct."

"Tell me, Dr. Stone," asked Charlotte wide-eyed in alarm. In spite of the deep pink blush that had wildly mounted in her face, "do you see Ezra Weeks ahead of us yonder? Look quickly at the bend of the road."

"I don't see a soul, Miss Charlotte. Are you uneasy over that ambling specimen of humanity?"

"I am so uneasy, I hesitate to call him anything with that much dignity."

"Forget it; that is the best thing to do, or I will begin to fear you are developing a case of nerves."

"Maybe so—but you know, Doctor, that man carries a dreadful feeling about with him. I feel when in his presence as though he carried enclosed within him a raging something bent on destruction. Do you feel that way too?"

"I should say not," laughed the doctor heartily. "Why, my dear, I shall have to tell your father of this so he can dismiss the fellow—it is not good for you to come in contact with such angular personalities."

"I wish you would," murmured Charlotte thoughtfully, more to herself than to the doctor. "I wish you would—he makes me feel so creepy, I actually shiver."

It was dusk when a little later they turned into the Madison's lane. Becky was swinging lazily in a hammock underneath the giant walnut trees. She wore a soft cool flowered voile dress and a magazine she had been reading was thrown on the grass. Andy, in light trousers and white shirt, was stretched upon the grass at her feet, his head upon a cushion. Andy jumped up quickly when he saw the doctor and Charlotte approaching.

"Bless me, if the doctor isn't stealing my girl away from me." he laughed gaily, taking Charlotte's hands.

"I would have to work like the old mischief, you young scamp," rejoined the doctor merrily. "Can't you thank me for rescuing her for you, from an evening of loneliness on a lovely moonlight night like this?" Doctor Stone, with a charming twinkle in his eyes, smiled quickly at Becky and with airy eloquence, lightly waved his hand.

"I certainly do, my dear fellow, a thousand thanks!"

"This is the most beautiful time of all the year, Andy, a summer night, a perfect moon, a river like a sunken mirror—by Jove, there ought to be a rowboat handy."

"This is, there is."

"Where, pray?"

"Just up the river a little way."

"Whose is it?"

"It is ours, my dear doctor, it is ours." Andy smiled broadly and they playfully shook hands.

"Let's go then!" exclaimed the doctor enthusiastically.

"When we come back," laughed Becky, "we will have a bonfire under the trees down there by the river and fix us something good to eat. I'll run and tell Mother we are going. I'll be back in a second."

With a light step, Becky was out of the hammock and across the lawn to her mother on the porch.

Soon the young people strolled away across the lawn and out into the quiet dark of the river road, beneath the intertwining branches of the tall forest trees. Charlotte and Andy fell behind, but soon came forward to lead the way. Dr. Stone lightly took Becky's arm to guide her through the dark. Somewhere in the deep woods of birches and elms along the banks of the ravine they were passing, a whippoorwill sang plaintively. The crickets were having a grand chorus, with every fiddle bowing merrily. The world to Becky seemed lost in one sweet song. It was a night for lovers and as is often the case where true love flows, the stream was wide and deep—the inadequacy of words being drowned in the overflowing surge. Each knew the other loved but still the doctor did not speak.

Everyone was surprised to see all at once the lights of a motor car loom over and down the hill beyond them, then quickly slow down and go out.

"There is something wrong, don't you think, Andy," asked Charlotte, "about that car?"

"I would not worry, dear, no doubt it is a couple of lovers, this is Lover's Lane, you know."

"Yes, but Andy—Manning was going to meet Ezra tonight somewhere—I just feel it can't be any other way—do you suppose that is him?"

"My, but you do carry a big burden of worry over me."

"Don't laugh, silly—I think I hear someone talking."

Andy and Charlotte waiting for Dr. Stone and Becky. Through the soft night came the lowered tones of men's voices.

"It is somebody, sure as I live!" breathed Andy in alarm. "I'm going up there to find out what is up."

"We will all go with you," entreated Charlotte. "Becky and I will hide beside the road."

Night had settled down in earnest. Only in midstream on the river could the light from the moon be seen hanging like a gossamer veil. The party came to a standstill and concealed themselves behind a huge clump of elderberries. Again they heard the lowered tones of men's voices. They seemed to be approaching. Becky and Charlotte could make out the shape of a large truck alongside the fence at the woods' edge. In a short time, they saw two figures appear carrying something. They were presently aware of the ominous clink of bottles in case after case of illicit liquor, being lifted over the fence and carefully deposited in the back of the truck.

When Andy perceived what was going on and saw the slouched form of Ezra Weeks going back and forth in the darkness, he felt an uncontrollable desire to step right out and demand by what right they could manufacture and deliver that hateful stuff from his place. Dr. Stone felt him start forward, but seeing that the two men were armed, laid a firm hand on his shoulder, pulling him back with a determined hold.

When the loading ceased, a short conversation began which was quite audible.

"The boss said to hurry back. You get the rest of the dough, Ez, when you finish the job. Get busy!"

"They'd agone the fust time if thet damn hog doctor hadn't come along!"

"Do as you're told—that's all you got to do if you want the jack!"

"When's the boss a comin' this way?"

"In a day or two—now git out—I'm goin'."

Dr. Stone and Andy gently pushed the girls into the denser shade of the elderberries and sank back out of sight as the powerful lights of the truck started up. The heavily loaded machine was backed up, turned around, and driven off at a lively speed. In the darkness which immediately closed down, nothing was heard or seen of Ezra. Like a phantom, had silently disappeared in the dense woods covering the ravine.

After waiting a proper length of time the party of young folks came out onto the road, the girls frightened and the entire group's attitude that of angry hornets.

"I don't know how in blazes, you all feel!" exploded Andy, "but I am so consarned mad, my boat ride is gone up the river!"

"Same here," said the doctor, "Andy, we had better get back to the house."

"He means to clean me out, one way or another." Andy's tone was bitter.

"It is better now we know a little of what is going on." Charlotte added gently, "I think we had better hurry home, don't you, Becky?"

"Yes, Mother is all alone, come on, let's hurry!" she answered anxiously.

"If I found any hogs in shape in the morning, I would sell them, Andy," advised the doctor. "If you don't, he will somehow get the rest. I wish it was tomorrow right now!"

"So do I!" agreed everyone, almost in unison.

The road that was once taken so leisurely was now traversed quickly. Arriving home, Becky led the way to the house.

"It seems so good to be where there is a light once more," she began cheerfully. "I hate tricks like that and it is hard to love the people who pull them off. They make me think of those sour bugs I sometimes find under old stones in our garden; they love the darkness and run from the light."

"I think we had better take a turn over the barn-lot and around the house, don't you think, Andy?" queried the doctor.

"Now," laughed Charlotte, "who has developed a case of nerves?"

"Believe me!" replied the doctor, "I wouldn't give that reptile an inch if I can help it!"

"Neither do you grace him with membership in the tribe of humanity," teased Charlotte.

"No, I don't!" replied the doctor dryly. "I see now what you mean, Miss Charlotte, about that vague something he possesses. It is not tangible, yet it has the power to make the flesh crawl. Come on, Andy, let's have a look around."

Lucy had gone to bed and left the light on in the kitchen, so while the doctor and Andy were gone, Charlotte and Becky prepared some food to eat and set the table. They laid a lovely rose and blue bordered cloth, set the table with paper plates and napkins, then put on a delicious lunch of cold sliced beef tongue, cottage cheese, bread and butter pickles, strawberry jam, and salt-rising bread. Becky was bringing in a huge blue earthenware pitcher of cold buttermilk when the men returned.

"Did you see or hear anything out of the way?" asked Charlotte, putting the chairs up to the table.

"Not a sight or a sound" – answered Andy, "but just the same I have a hunch I ought to sleep in the barn tonight."

"Come, let's sit down and eat," said Becky happily. "I'd like to forget all this for a moment. Charlotte, sit here, and the men can find their own places, please."

The little lunch was just getting started when the kitchen seemed to become quite rosy all of a sudden. It was a queer reddish glow that caused the heart to stand still, the lips refused to move, and the hands to frantically clutch the throat.

"My God!" moaned Andy, springing up and backing his chair away so suddenly it turned over. "The barn's on fire!"

With another cry of piercing agony, Andy had disappeared followed by Dr. Stone. Everything turned black to Becky. She hurried after them and halted by the door jam feeling faint. In the screen door to the porch, the girls leaned against one another, horror smitten at the sight of the once beautiful white and gray barn — a huge three storied affair — silhouetted against the roaring flames within; every board black and every scarlet crack revealed. The hissing and crackling of the flames, leaping and shriveling the hay and timbers as they went, completely sickened the girls in a drowning sense of fear.

Only an instant they stood thus, then as if awakened by an electric shock, they ran to the milk house for the buckets, frantically talking to each other.

"They'll never save the barn now," wailed Becky. "It's a blaze from top to bottom."

"Maybe we can help save the corn cribs," cried Charlotte, the tears running down her cheeks unchecked. "If the cribs go, everything goes!"

Running to the barn-lot, the girls found Andy and the doctor laboring like stricken animals in the quivering heat between the barn and the scorching corn cribs. It was as Becky said — the barn was completely given over to the flames and every effort was being made to save the double cribs to keep the house from going. The water was getting low in the horse tank and the gasoline engine was not working to pump it, only by fitful jerks and starts.

A rush of wind lifted the burning shingles from the huge barn roof – where the timbers gleamed in warped agony, and sent them in a brilliant shower accompanied by myriads of sparks, over the cribs, past the milk house, and on to the precious old home.

With a terrible cry of anguish and deep despair, Becky cried aloud, forgetful of every human close to hear.

"Oh Father – it's an outrageous attempt to burn us out! Oh hear my prayer, Father – turn the wind the same as you parted the Red Sea!"

Tears streamed down Becky's cheeks in bitterness. She was beside herself, and feeling a sense of utter helplessness – she clenched her small delicate hands and dumbly shifted her weight from one numb foot to the other. Being insensible to everything but the certain onrush of the hungry flames, her lips continued to move in whispered prayer while she saw, with horror stricken eyes, the roof of the milk house catch on fire.

The wind rose higher and carried another huge lurid fan of shingles from the fast disappearing barn roof into the sky. Without waiting to see the effect of it, Becky started to run to the house, thinking to awaken her mother and begin saving what she could from the house.

She was startled and comforted to find the yard and lane fast filling up with automobiles from which people began to tumble like rats from a sinking boat. Her course was intercepted by the crowd which came running at the sight of her with a thousand questions on anxious lips. Only the women remained, the men hastening on to those who labored so frantically to save the corn cribs.

"Any stock in the barn?" asked a large, imposing woman. Becky and Charlotte stood together wide-eyed and speechless. Becky felt that she would scream if the crowd didn't part and let her through to her mother.

"Any stock in the barn!" demanded the woman again.

"No, all in the orchard," mumbled Becky and the answer was carried from lip to lip through the crowd.

"It's a darn good thing the wind wuz blowin' t' the other way," remarked a peculiar little woman in a gray calico dress, "or you'd be without anything at all."

Becky realized then that the wind had really turned and that the milk-house roof was no longer in flames. With heartfelt joy and fervent gratitude, Becky's lips moved once more in a prayer to her Creator for turning the tide.

"It's a goin'! Look out everbodie!" Roared a deep voice in the dense crowd which instinctively fell back a pace.

With a creaking followed by a moment of intense breathlessness, the top timbers, naked and already charred, swayed – paused – then crashed loose at either end, making a huge cave-in, in the center of the barn, and followed by the ends of the barn crashing simultaneously with the center beams. The hay, long burnt to a smoldering bed, received the charred timber and fire mounted anew to the sky in a veritable fountain. The heat became so intense and furious, the light seemed reflected in a shimmering cloud between the fascinated onlookers and the gleaming furnace. There is that about fire which has the awfulness of death. Both hold the onlooker helpless and fill the breast with dumb misery.

The last vestige of any outlines of the fallen timbers had ceased to be and only the blackened cracked rock foundation reared itself in mute humility to the tragedy, when Becky, still holding fast to Charlotte's hand, turned to work her way through the dense crowd to the house. She found the porch surrounded and they passed through with difficulty. Softly the girls mounted the spacious old carved stairway and Becky found her mother resting in deep slumber. Her even breathing breaking the stillness of the room.

Deeply thankful that her mother had been spared the sight of the ordeal, Becky and Charlotte tip-toed from the room. When they returned to the yard they saw that the terrible heat from the barn had caused the leaves on the old walnut tree over the milk-house to scorch and curl.

The automobiles began to go and before fifteen minutes were passed the old lane was left to cheerlessness. As if fascinated, the girls leaned on the barnyard rail fence and watched the fading embers glow and glow afresh, with every passing breeze, then lose themselves in the parched darkness.

Presently they saw four figures coming toward them, dirty beyond description, bedraggled, weary, and covered with grimy perspiration. The girls recognized George Hudnut, Tom Pendelton, Dr. Stone, and Andy. Of all the weary figures, Andy's seemed the most exhausted. It seemed as if ten years had been added to him in the few short moments since the disaster. The girls listened as they came striding forward, glad of the sound of familiar voices.

"Great Scot!" boomed out George Hudnut in astonishment, "the old walnut over the milk house is sure scorched!"

"Oh, everything wuz dryer than a powder horn. It's a wonder the hull place didn't go." Tom Pendelton pulled out an excessively dirty red bandanna and blew his ample nose like a foghorn.

"No water hardly in the well, no buckets, or ladders handy – I sure am a dunce," Andy's voice was a doleful whisper.

"Cheer up, Andy, old fellow, the work we did was faster than the blazes." Dr. Stone's powerful hand came down in a courageous clasp of brotherliness.

"My gracious," grasped Becky getting a good view of the quartet by the aid of the porch light. "If I hadn't known you had been fighting fires – I'd believe this was a coal mine you'd been working in!"

"It looks to me like someone might be hurt," said Charlotte anxiously.

"You men go over to the bench by the smokehouse there and Charlotte and I will bring a tub of water, towels and soap. What you need, everyone of you, is a good scrub and something to eat before you go home."

"Somethin' to eat!" exclaimed Tom Pendelton, beginning to get ready to wash. "Lord, I could eat a barrel o' salt mackerel!"

A slim figure in a lavender kimono appeared in the door of the screen porch. "Oh my children, whatever has happened – is anyone hurt?"

"No, no, Mother dear," cried Andy, taking her in his arms, "we are all right, everyone of us – but the old barn is gone."

Becky and Charlotte appeared with the tub and towels, then took Lucy into the living room and told her all about it. Lucy listened with tears in her eyes.

"I am afraid we have enemies, my dears," was her only comment.

The men came in and Becky and Charlotte fixed fresh places for them. After a short grace, Tom Pendelton said forcefully–

"It's a dirty shame this had to happen – but there is going to be some fun before long or my name is not Pendelton!"

"I think we had all better go right away to town and get the sheriff to make out the warrants!"

"That is a good idea, George," added Dr. Stone.

"Let's go then," roared George. "I'm jes achin' ter see this here fight finished. Nobody had better try stoppin' me when I get started – I'm rearin' ter go."

"Andy can stay here and rest till mornin' – lookin' after the women folks. I guess, Charlotte, you'll have to stay all night. Ain't much tellin' when we will be pullin' in." Tom Pendelton spoke decisively and arose from the table, followed by the doctor and George. They chatted a bit to Andy on the porch, then stepped out into the night.

Andy and the girls came in to see their mother after the three good friends had left the house. He sat down on the old couch in the spacious living room and bowed his head, his elbows on his knees, his forehead buried in his hands.

"Oh Mother," Andy's voice broke in despair. "We are completely ruined. The hogs will all die and the barn is gone."

"Don't say that, my boy." Lucy came and put her loving hands on his shoulders. "We have lost heavily but we are not ruined. We have no hogs, we have no barn, and it looks like we will eventually have no farm – but my dear, we are far from ruined."

"I don't get you, Mother?" Andy raised a haggard face.

"Haven't we just as many friends as we ever had, dear, haven't we here each other, haven't we just as much love as ever, and haven't we just as much determination to labor and keep going as we ever had? Ah – my boy – we have lost heavily tonight – but let us not say we are ruined. We have only lost the temporal things. Are we not blessed with the dear Gospel? What does it teach us? My dear son, from now on we must never look backward in sorrow or vain regrets. Let us trust in the Lord and do good. He will yet bring all the desires of our hearts to pass. Cheer up and let us set ourselves with a will to be happy – to do happy things and forget the shadows around us. I am sure Heavenly Father loves us just as much as ever and who knows but what all this tribulation is for the best?"

"That sounds good, Mother, to hear you speak with so much hope and courage."

"Well, Andy, I've lived many years, and the older I get the more I learn to appreciate trouble. This has blessed me with sympathy and charity for my neighbors, and often it has driven me to the throne of grace. If it had not been so–I 'm afraid I would scarcely know our Heavenly Father,

"Sit down, Mother darling, you are a treasure to me. Here–sit right beside me. Charlotte can sit on the little footstool on your side and Becky can sit on the one on my side after she has brought me my Book of Mormon."

Becky went over to the library table and brought back a beautiful volume bound in handsome black morocco. Andy quickly turned the gilt-edged India paper leaves and came at last to a little past the center of the book.

"There, Mother darling, read it to us, it is the eleventh chapter of III Nephi."

With quiet gentleness, Lucy took the beloved book and began to read. It was a passage they all loved but it was, of course, new to Charlotte. The soft tones of Lucy's well-poised voice fell like soothing music on their ruffled nerves. Gone was the terrible excitement of the fire and in its place came a sweetness that was impossible to express in earthly language.

Charlotte understood that it was an account of the appearance of the Savior after His crucifixion to the people she had never heard of before until recently. Was this an account of what happened when he came to that other fold he told the Jews of? Charlotte became enthralled in the beauty of the passages and drank the words in hungrily.

"And it came to pass as they understood, they cast their eyes up again towards heaven; and behold, they saw a man descending out of heaven; and he was clothed in a white robe, and he came down and stood in the midst of them, and the eyes of the whole multitude were turned upon him, and they durst not open their mouths, even one to another, and wist not what it meant, for they thought it was an angel that had appeared unto them.

"And it came to pass that he stretched forth his hand and spake unto the people, saying,

"Behold, I am Jesus Christ, whom the prophets testified shall come into the world;

"And behold, I am the light and the life of the world; and I have drunk out of that bitter cup which the Father hath given me, and have glorified the Father in taking upon me the sins of the world, in the which I have suffered the will of the Father in all things from the beginning.

"And it came to pass that when Jesus had spoken these words, the whole multitude fell to the earth for they remembered that it had been prophesied among them that Christ should show himself unto them after his ascension into Heaven.

"And it came to pass that the Lord spake unto them saying--

"Arise and come forth unto me, that ye may thrust your hands into my side and also that ye may feel the prints of the nails in my hands and in my feet, that ye may know that I am the God of Israel, and the God of the whole earth, and have been slain for the sins of the world.

"And it came to pass that the multitude went forth and thrust their hands into his side, and did feel the prints of the nails in his hands and in his feet; and this they did do, going forth one by one, until they had all gone forth and did see with their eyes, and did feel with their hands, and did known of a surety, and did bear record, that it was he of whom it was written by the prophets that should come.

"And when they had all gone forth and had witnessed for themselves they did cry out with one accord, saying--

"Hosanna, blessed be the name of the Most High God! And they did fall down at the feet of Jesus and did worship him."

Charlotte was filled with a moving understanding that sensed the deep spiritual significance of each exalted phrase that caused Lucy's spirit to leap with joy—so that her very features were moved under the powerful testimony of the truthfulness of the words by the Holy Spirit within her. Tears came to the eye—and the gentle old voice quavered–but the spirit grew bold within and heavenly peace bathed the room as if the morning sun had once again shed its life-giving beams abroad.

Gone from Charlotte was the fear of which road she should take. She no longer stood by the sign which unhesitatingly pointed the way to Christ in a perplexing manner. Forgotten was every suspicious thought or bit of caution. Mentally she had taken a step down that self-same road and beheld with fascinated eyes the fact that although the road undoubtedly was narrow and straight, although there seemed to be few travelers upon it, the road eventually wound gently into the celestial hills. Ah—there lay the peace and contentment for which her soul so hungered. She saw that those who traveled that way were undoubtedly accompanied on the journey by the administering spirits. That their thoughts and emotions were lifted above those who traveled in the mazes that never led anywhere. She thirsted to know more of this wonderful story and without another backward look or thought of consequences, Charlotte cried out in joy as she moved forward.

"Oh Mother Madison, those are truly the most beautiful words I ever heard in my life—I believe they are true."

"Of course, deary," cried Lucy, softly as with arched eyebrows and slightly thrown back head—she peered gently through her old fashioned glasses at Charlotte. The tender words of confession brought tears of joy into the faded blue eyes—and a pair of wrinkled brown hands in happiness enclosed the girl's fair ones. "Of course, the words are true, and they are the most precious words on earth. They actually laid their hands on his side and on his hands and feet. What a glorious privilege and from one who had been through the gates of death!"

To Lucy, Andy, and Becky the precious passage brought a renewing of the light that was already lit. But to Charlotte it changed an already attractive countenance into a beautiful one. It seemed to the three who saw her that every trace of this world's expression had vanished and in its place came the soft radiance of the soul within forever more alight with the word of truth.

Tenderly, Andy drew Charlotte to him with a happy cry—

"God be thanked, no longer will I grieve over what I have lost of this world's goods. He has blessed me with that for which I prayed. I now have my truest blessing. Mother darling, we will all go West and start again."

Chapter 10 A perfect rattle-snake!

The morning sun was sending its shafts of light down through the walnut grove, when Elvira Hudnut got out of her car and came to the place where Lucy sat on the front porch, snapping green beans. Lucy had taken her work to the front of the house, so that she might not see the ruins of the old barn and enjoy the pleasure of the sight of the sparkling river to comfort her. She looked up kindly at Elvira's approach.

Elvira was agitated—"George has jes gone over to Pendeltons for some reason or other," she began. "I wanted him to stay and see if he couldn't find some trace of who did the mischief, but he jes wouldn't do it. Thet's a man fer ye!"

"I'd hate to think I had an enemy who disliked me so much as to burn my barn, Elvira—set down here in this old rocker. It is quite pleasant this morning."

"The dogs' hind-foot, Lucy Madison! We all have enemies, some dislike us more than others. Whoever did that is a perfect rattle-snake!"

Lucy looked closely at her dear old energetic friend, who now sat close beside her. Already Elvira's wrinkled old hands, brown and knotted, were beginning to snap beans too, the large veins standing out plainly above the tissues.

Kind old hands, thought Lucy. Somehow they reminded her of her father's hands. She felt a wave of sadness go over her. It was just such hands that made life worth living. When once they were gone, who else could take their place? A surge of appreciation for the love of her old friend swept over her.

"Yes," she replied kindly, "we all perhaps have enemies—but thank God we have friends too. Elvira, I have decided to take my children and go West."

"You mean out to thet Brigham Young country?"

"Yes, Elvira, that is where I belong, where I long to go, and where I mean to die."

"Well, if thet is the case, I'm goin' too, or my name ain't Elvira. I been thinkin' and studyin' about whut them elders say, and I believe they're right. I tuck the notion last night as I wuz alayin' in bed, thet I might jes as well be baptized right short off, seein' as them two books Elder Thorensen give me clenches the argument."

"What was the other book, Elvira?"

"The Book of Mormon—oh Lucy, thet's a fine book. T'ain't no use foolin' around here no longer. George, he wants to go too. He says whuts the use of havin' sech an all-fired mighty family-tree if we don't up and do somethin' with it. I figer he's right. Charlie says he will stay here, in case we don't like the climate and want t' come back, but he's goin' to be baptized with us. I think I have lots ter thank the good Lord fer."

The tears of joy were running down Lucy's cheeks, but Elvira never raised her eyes during her long speech. She continued to look through her silver-rimmed spectacles at the beans she snapped expertly.

"Oh Elvira," quavered Lucy, overcome, "do you really mean it?"

"Mean it? Demanded Elvira vigorously. "I should say I do! I don't give a continental about all them fool yarns we've been a hearin' fer lo these many years, about Brigham Young and his many wives. I jes says ter myself—What uv it? You ain't got no kick comin', Elvira. Hain't ye fer years swallered head, tail and all, all them stories in the Bible about Abraham, David and Solomon! Hit says in there thet they knew the Lord. I allus figered the Lord wuz the same yesterday, terday and ter-morrow, and I says ter myself if he had anything ter do with them reverend patriarchs, how come he'd snub Brigham Young fer follerin' in their footsteps?"

"Well, Elvira, the world don't think so—"

"No, the world don't think so, I guess hit don't! But I hain't lived these sixty odd years fer nothin'! The devil, he says, don't mind the Lord—er keep his ways—but go do as ye please. Did ye ever see human nature, when it gets thet idea under its roof, turn out anything but a rag-weed? They don't do thet way now out there, Lucy, but the unholy world ain't got rid uv the beams in hits own eyes yet. Leastwise they continue to sling jeers yet about thet part uv the faith. But God ain't never yet called the man er woman uv their stamp ter serve him. He wants the valiant ones! Seems like time has been hangin' so heavy like on my hands fer years, I ain't hed nuthin' ter do but jes piddle around waitin' fer somethin'. I guess hit wuz this here religion, I needed it to add the pepper-sauce to my life. I ain't able ter git out and work like I use ter do. George, he says, I'll jes be fixed fer a good many years o' happiness workin' in thet Temple. When I think uv all them folks o' mine awaitin' all these years fer my family ter wake up, I don't see why the long sufferin' o' God Almighty didn't jes git plum exhausted!"

"That is what I want to do too, Elvira. We planned to buy a little place out in the country not far from Salt Lake City; then I could go back and forth, see, to the Temple each day or so."

"Thet is a grand idea!" nodded Elvira approvingly. "Maybe my George will do somethin' like thet too. He never wuz no man fer town."

Both women looked up from their work at the sound of a motor driving up the lane. The handsome car stopped close to the house in the shade of the walnuts. Lucy's heart sank with dismay when she saw John Manning's heavy dapper figure coming toward her from around the corner of the house.

Elvira's mouth fell open in astonishment. The much cherished salt and pepper wig slipped dangerously back over her ears, as she gave her head a vigorous toss. Its appearance gave her an extremely high forehead and a dignified air.

"Confound this contraption!" she muttered disapprovingly, hastily tilting it back into place and furtively looking to see if her act was seen. With a stiffened air, she straightened up and diligently resumed her bean-snapping.

Poor Lucy kept her eyes on her work steadfastly. Her fingers trembled in spite of herself over the long green beans. She heard Manning stop and knew that he stood directly in front of her at the foot of the steps.

"Good morning, Mrs. Madison, how are you today?"

Manning spoke in his most affable manner, gracefully tipping his hat to her. Lucy had never seen a man bear himself with so much poise. She felt like the insignificant bit of burnt paper which glowed and faded on the end of his cigarette. She was filled with extreme bitterness and a sickly fear. In her dilemma she knew not which way to turn and piteously showed her mental attitude in spite of a fierce struggle to subdue her emotions.

"Very well, thank you." she answered.

"I see you have had a fire recently."

"Yes, last night."

"How strange, spontaneous maybe."

"I'm sure I don't know." Lucy's delicate voice trailed off rather wistfully. Manning smiled queerly and, taking more assurance unto himself than ever, said very business-like.

"I am sorry to inform you, Mrs. Madison, but the payment on your mortgage is overdue. The company is in no position at present to carry the matter further. A payment is expected today!"

"Why," grasped Lucy, completely astonished, "I thought I had a few days left."

Manning smiled significantly and his loose mouth curled in a sneer. He watched her closely from the corner of his small dark eyes, much as a cat watches a mouse it has caught, wounded, then freed for a moment only.

Elvira saw with ready mounting anger the plight of her dearest friend. The anguish that gripped Lucy's heart weighed heavily on her own, tugging at her mercilessly. Seeing that Lucy was at her breaking point, unable to speak as her chin quivered so, Elvira was moved to the depths. She felt her veins grow dangerously hot and a queer clutching sensation crept around her throat, then in uncontrollable righteous wrath, she burst out—

"Hain't ye a little early with this business, Manning?" she questioned sarcastically, eyeing him narrowly.

Surprised, Manning looked at her as though she was entirely out of her place. He turned his head contemptuously and at once addressed Lucy bluntly.

"If you are in no position to make a payment, Mrs. Madison—I shall foreclose immediately!"

With a swish and a whirl, like dry leaves caught in a small whirlwind, Elvira rose to her feet, a tall angular, yet commanding figure in her extremely full long gray dress. She planted herself immediately in front of Lucy— between her friend and Manning's bulldog face.

"To whom air ye speakin'?" she demanded in a tone of authority.

Manning, seeing trouble in store, laughed lightly and looked triumphantly up into her wrinkled countenance.

"I am here to speak to the owner of this place—not you! Please step aside, Madam!"

"If thet be the case then, ye will jes have ter continue talking' ter the party in front uv ye!"

"Hell woman! What d' you mean?" said Manning.

"Jes what I said! "This here place is mine! My lawyer will call at your office this afternoon and settle this matter once and fer all. Now hits high time them dandy legs o' your'n wuz movin' off these here premises as fast as they kin waddle!"

Manning stared at her, a blank expression on his coarse face. His mouth was open in dumb astonishment.

"Move, I tell ye–" snorted Elvira, descending a step and shaking her knotted old fist under his nose. "Git! Ye do as I tell ye!"

Manning, crestfallen and speechless, backed away as she advanced with Lucy at her heels, then broke into an agitated shamble around the corner of the house.

"There's the bird, grab him, fellars!" roared out Andy's excited voice.

Elvira and Lucy ran to the side yard. Their eyes fell upon the already besieged figure of Manning, surrounded by George Hudnut, Dr. Stone, and Andy. Becky and Charlotte came tumbling out of the front door to see the excitement. They joined Elvira and Lucy who were as much aroused as an old hen with chicks is over a spreading-viper.

"Look at that hound, will ye," hissed Elvira, pointing a long bony finger past the group of men holding Manning tightly.

There stood Tom Pendelton, grasping by the shirt collar, the scare-crow form of none other than Ezra Weeks. Fear was written on every line of his body and his knees trembled so he could scarcely hold himself together.

With a dangerous shove, Andy marched Manning over to the bedraggled Carolinian.

"Did you ever see that fellow before?" he demanded sternly.

"I never did!" blustered Manning. "Get out of my way, I'm going!" He started off and was collared again by the powerful arm of young Andy.

"There now," mocked George Hudnut, grinning wickedly at Manning's elbow. "Jes take hit easy like—so you ain't never seen this bird before. Well, well, thet's strange. Ye've seen him, ain't ye, Ez?"

Ezra looked up dully, then shifted his watery blue eyes sheepishly.

"He come ter see me, told me whut ter do and I done it," he muttered.

"Is that so, Manning?" demanded Dr. Stone.

"No, it isn't – let me go I say!"

Manning glared like an angry bull at Andy and threw up his heavy hairy fist menacingly. Andy only grinned broadly and tightened his hold on Manning's shirt collar until the perspiration burst out on his face. Manning squared himself dangerously for battle but with a mighty shake that completely shook the back-bone out of Manning, Andy declared to him in cool even tones--

"Keep still, Manning. The federal officers will be here in a moment. Anything you may do or say very likely will be used against you."

"Federal officers! What do you mean? Let me go I tell you – I've not done anything. This is a matter you'll suffer for, young man. The idea – of federal officers after a man of my standing and prestige! Let me go – or I'll – "

"That is enough out of you," blazed Andy straightforwardly. "You know perfectly well you caused my hogs to have cholera – you had the barn burned, you had that despicable still planted on my property and all because you wanted this place. You were determined I should never pay that mortgage off and was so sure of it – you actually had the nerve to begin to use my place for the evil purposes you wanted it for, before it really fell into your hands."

Manning made a wild lunge to get free of Andy's determined grasp.

"Stay right where you are, Manning," commanded Andy sternly, "the officers will be here and take you in charge – I have an idea instead of me going over the road as you planned, it is your turn now."

"Here they are now," cried Tom Pendelton excitedly.

With the keenest of interest, everyone's eyes turned toward the fast approaching new-comers. Suddenly without warning, Dr. Stone cried and sprang forward–

"He'll shoot, look out, boys!"

George Hudnut and Andy instantly grasped the situation and with Dr. Stone grappled fiercely with the desperate man. Becky and Charlotte unconsciously gave a startled scream. Lucy, stern faced and white to the lips, followed Elvira forward to where the men struggled in determination to wrench the weapon from the man's iron hold.

With a mighty heave like the force put forth by a brute beast, Manning turned his arm inwardly beneath his bowed form and shot. A convulsive shudder passed through his huge body and instantly all hands escaped him and he fell lifeless.

A moan of despair swept over the little body of people. The officers parted them and silently bent down and examined the now lifeless body.

"My lord," exclaimed Andy, the first to find his voice, "a suicide!"

The blood was fast staining the elegant silk shirt and handsome coat which Manning wore. In his pudgy right hand he still grasped the deadly revolver. A very small neat affair in German silver.

"He was a bird that flew entirely too high," said the strange young officer.

"The dirty dog," flared Tom Pendelton disgustedly. "Look at that, Ez." He gave Ezra a heathen-ish shake. "Do you see that! He couldn't face his own music. You're in a nice mess!"

"I allus did say that man wuz a sneakin' rattle-snake." said Elvira, her mouth drawn up in a thin straight determined line, "an now he's gone and proved hit. The idee --"

"Yep," amended George. "He's jes like a reptile thet is cornered. If he can't escape, he strikes himself."

"Death is a terrible solemn thing," Lucy added faintly. "Oh it's sad to see such a sight. How could he face his reward?"

"That guy never lived for a reward, Madam," remarked a sedate senior officer. "He believed in neither Heaven nor Hell."

"In other words," said Tom Pendelton decisively, "he was a complete fool."

"You are right, sir, he lived for nothing but gain and pleasure. He was a bad one."

"Yeah," agreed the younger officer, "and he sure made the dough. We knew he was the mastermind of a gigantic white slave and bootleg ring all over three states with headquarters in Hammond. But it was hard to get the goods on him. Good thing, Stone, you got the license number on that truck last night."

"Let's be going Carter," urged the other officer, "we have lots to do now. Get that fellow over there from Pendelton. Put him in the front seat of our car and if you fellows will give me a lift with this—we'll be off."

The officer bent over and took a shoulder of the body. George stepped forward and took the other, while Tom Pendelton lifted the heavy legs and feet. They carried their burden and deposited it on the back seat of the officer's car, directly behind the huddled form of Ezra.

After a command from the officer to bring in Manning's car and one of their own to return in, the cars were soon out onto the quiet river road, leaving the silent group of women to watch their departure, with the shock of the deed that had passed before their eyes written clearly on their faces.

"Oh Mother, wasn't that terrible?" Becky spoke wide-eyed in a numb way. "To think he would kill himself here at our house—before our very eyes."

"Shucks, Becky," exclaimed Elvira, "sech a man hain't got no respect fer people ner places. He's jes like the Bible describes a violent man and he died jes like one."

"Yes, Elvira," nodded Lucy. "He was a violent man. He lived like the man who said there was no God."

"Land sakes, let's get out of here, this blood makes us all sick—we'd better git in the house and start readin' a book or somethin'," said Elvira vigorously. "I feel kinder faint myself and ye all look as white as sheets."

They turned and started back to the house.

"It's hot, Elvira," said Lucy, "I don't want to go into the house. Let's sit here on the steps."

"Yes, do, Mother," said Becky, "I'll go get the gingerbread I baked this morning and some fresh buttermilk from the cellar."

Lucy looked up at Elvira from where she sat and inquired meekly—

"Whatever did you mean, Elvira, by telling him you owned this place? I'm afraid that don't help me any."

"Lucy, ain't you never learned yet—I'm the most cheerful liar on earth?"

Elvira looked out of the corner of her faded gray eyes, a humorous smile coming and going over her old face.

"You should never have done it for me, Elvira—never."

"Lucy Madison, jes give me one good reason why I shouldn't buy this place fer my son Charlie. Ain't he jes achin' ter marry Ellen Thatcher and settle down? Ain't I been a wearin' these old style clothes fer years and years, a savin' my money? I'm gitten tired uv takin' hit ter the bank! Land sakes, ain't ye goin' to sell out anyway?"

"Yes," objected Lucy weakly, "but Charlie will want an extremely modern place with plenty of barn room."

"Don't you worry there, dearie, this place is jes what Charlie needs. He allus has had new fangled notions about barns and old fangled ones about houses. Now is the chance ter try 'em out and see whut they are worth. Besides he says he is tired uv advertising them Pollen

179

China hogs 'o his in the papers and magazines–and wants a place out closer ter the road to express his ideas in thet direction too."

"Then you think he will be satisfied with this place?"

"Of course he would. He's been a wantin' ter marry Sarie Thatcher's girl fer the last two years, but Sarie jes wouldn't hear uv hit 'cause my place was so terribly Victorian. As fer this place hit would jes suit Ellen!"

Becky and Charlotte appeared with the gingerbread and buttermilk. They graciously gave each old lady a plate and glass, then spread some blue checked linen napkins on their laps.

"Elvira says she wants to buy our home, Becky, for Charlie."

"Oh, do you think you would really be satisfied with it, Aunt Elvira? Maybe you had better consider it a bit farther."

"I tell ye whut I'll do," said Elvira determinedly—"I'll give ye exactly whut ye consider the place worth, stock, machinery, household furniture, and all. Thet will save ye a sale, Lucy. I hate sales. They are one of the most exasperatin' things I know uv. Everbodie prowlin' around tryin' ter buy somethin' fer nothin', jes like women at bargain counters. Ellen is jes as crazy as ye air over colonial furniture—she haz been bit by one uv them collectin' bugs too. I got some old blue home-spun coverlets over there she is jest wild over."

"Then the place will certainly be yours, Elvira. I'd rather it went into Charlie's hands than anyone I know. He is a hustler and as long as he has it, it will look good. Andy can go into town right away with him and settle the business. I will talk to him about the price as soon as he comes back and we will make it right for you. Then we will pay off that mortgage and go west. You'd better come and go out there when we go, Elvira."

"No, I think I'll wait a little bit—I got so much business ter attend to and I want ter look around a bit. But whut ye say leaves me satisfied, Lucy. I think ye had all better come over tomorrow night ter our baptism service."

"Are you going to be baptized tomorrow night, Mrs. Hudnut?" cried Charlotte happily. "Oh Mother Madison, why can't I be too and be all ready then to go west with you?"

"You could, dearie, if your parents are willing," gently answered Lucy. "The elders will not stay much longer with Elvira—they are about done tracting around here."

"If thet is the way the wind hez been blowin', young lady," said Elvira delightedly, "come over—an welcome. Sounds ter me like a weddin' wuz in the air, Lucy!"

Chapter 11 The Spanking

Jane stood a moment inside the door of Charlotte's room with her slender jeweled hand on the doorknob. She looked around upon the beautiful neatness with a sneer and her anger flamed anew at the realization that although her room was furnished thrice more elegantly than this gentle domain—yet it had not the beauty and charm. A surge of jealousy swept over her again at the remembrance of the sight of Charlotte and Dr. Stone walking off together. Somehow, every scheme of her life failed. The things she always deeply wanted were either beyond her reach, or they had a way of slipping through her fingers, leaving her heart hungry and chagrined. It never occurred to her that the lack was on her part. She diligently blamed the other person.

"It's always the same," she complained bitterly. "Take this room for instance. There isn't a single piece of furniture in my room but what cost more than this whole outfit; but this miserable stuff looks better than mine. I wonder how she does it? Look how she set me back at dinner, too. I've much more education than she has— I've been out more—but I don't seem to be able to hold my own there either. I can't for the life of me see what could interest that handsome doctor in her. She isn't half as good looking as I am, just a green country girl. But with a charm about her that's hard to ignore. The kind of simple beauty that grows the more you see it.

It's like she doesn't even try to impress--but there you go! Oh I'm so mad I could scream!"

With a contemptible jerk at a quilted white satin pillow on the beautifully crocheted bedspread, she sent it flying across the room and displaced the shade of Charlotte's reading lamp.

Not having intended to disfigure Charlotte's little haven when she entered—her aim was more to stealthily search for any secrets she might uncover—the deliberate plan soon appealed to her beyond all her ability to resist. Like a ferocious little terrier, she immediately set about completely wrecking the perfect order of the little bedroom.

She marched over to the delicately draped dressing table and, with nervous fingers, sent the toilet articles, perfume, powder, and accessories helter-skelter. The full box of powder turned upside down on the colorful braided rug in front of the table. The drapery flew up rudely, and the neatly kept drawers beneath sprang open, spilling their lavender-scented contents wildly onto the rug. The large easy chair by the reading lamp was tilted back – its soft, broad cushion, she jerked out of place and threw with a vengeance into the beautiful flower box of salmon-pink geraniums, blooming luxuriantly in the soft twilight, crushing three-fourths of them outright. The airy, stenciled, ruffled curtains were the next to suffer a severe chastening, leaving them dangling from the parted rod and draped onto the floor.

Fully launched on her tirade of destruction, Jane, with hilarity in her surging tide of anger, sprang with alacrity toward the closet door and threw it open. Everything here was in the most beautiful order. The place was immaculate. The shelves were bound by the most charming pleated scallops, made from quaintly flowered chintz and bound in black. The stacks of undies and linen were tied with fascinating bows of the same material, all bound in the same way. The slippers were resting in their holders on the back of the door. Charlotte's simple little hats found repose on the top shelf on their hand-decorated holders. Jane surveyed the meager amount of frocks; old, but neatly mended and in perfect order on their cleverly padded hangers. The sight of the beauty, thoughtfulness and success of the closet made her furious. She remembered her own place for like things and stamped her small foot in rage. Now completely blind and beyond all control, she tore the simple frocks from their places—scattered them also on the floor, tearing this and ripping that beyond repair. The hats, slippers, and beautiful arranged shelves found the same fate. A box of much cherished papers and pictures fell to the floor, through which she looked eagerly for letters from Andy, thinking perchance she might have the fun of reading them. Chagrined in not finding anything, she turned and left the closet, stepping over all the things she had scattered on the floor.

The idea flashed into her mind that no doubt love letters were hidden under the mattress of the bed. With a flurry, off came the spread—the quilts, the sheets, and pillows. These she promiscuously tossed on the floor among the other scattered articles. The mattress was quite heavy, but with effort, she turned it back halfway at the head. Not finding anything, she made a thorough search by displacing the foot of the mattress also. A small neatly bound black book with gold letters on it met her eye. Full of curiosity, she snatched it up and read the title--

"The Book of Mormon!"

"Of all the brazen things," she exclaimed, hardly daring to believe her eyes. "What will Mother say? I wonder if she has any more of this stuff hid around. I'll see. Good thing I found it out—the little deceiving wretch!"

Clutching her surprising find in her hand, and with every suspicion aroused as to any conceivable hiding place, she began to tear up the only remaining orderly thing, the rug. With little gusts of laughter, she gleefully gathered into her hands the pamphlets Andy had given Charlotte on the beauties of Mormonism; from out the pages of one, which was now so rudely shaken, there fell the tender love letter. This she quickly read without a blush, ending with a cruel sneer on her hard perfect features.

"This is too good to be true!" she whispered. "Wait until I tell Mother and Father—they won't have her around any longer. The little saint! She won't dare to try to lord it over me again!"

Not stopping to survey the entire wreck she had made of her sister's room, Jane stepped blithely across the things on the floor, catching her feet in Charlotte's best party frock, rending it with reckless disregard, and rushed out into the hall, down the stairs into the sitting room to find her mother. She found no one. During her time in the bedroom, she had not been where she could see the sky with its red flare caused by the fire at the Madisons. Neither had she heard her mother and aunt leave the place.

Wondering where they were, she returned to her own room and sat down to look over the books she had found. The longer she read the more her fury arose.

At length, her body began to grow less tense from the nervous strain which her outburst had imposed upon it and her mind. Became sleepy from the contents of the Book of Mormon. Not having the Holy Spirit to set her mind aflame over its adventures, she fell asleep before she was aware of it. It was the middle of the night when she awoke and found all the folks asleep. Silently she went to bed and when she awoke the morning was far advanced.

Dressing quickly, she slipped downstairs to find her mother; Cora was resting in a big overstuffed chair, reading. At the sight of Jane's appearance, Cora looked up rather lazily, but seeing the excitement on her face, she inquired quickly–

"For pity sakes, what is it?"

"Look at this, Mother," said Jane righteously.

"Look at what?"

"This Book of Mormon and this other trash!" Out fell Dr. Penrose's treatise on "Why I Became a Mormon" into Cora's lap from the back of the volume of Nephite literature.

"For the love of—"

"Yes, I should say! She had it hid away, just like a common little sneak."

"Who?"

"Charlotte!"

"She has! Well, it's high time this was stopped!"

"I found it under the mattress—the papers were under the rug!"

"Why the brazen thing," exclaimed Cora, thoroughly provoked. "I'll show her a thing or two! Why, it's a rank disgrace to the Pendelton family—going on like this!"

"What's up now?" inquired Aunt Em, sticking her head inquisitively through the kitchen door into the cool dining room.

"Em, enough to make me a gray-headed overnight!" declared Cora, vigorously banging her handful of the hateful papers down on the broad arm of her chair until the dust flew.

"Land sakes!" exclaimed Em, coming into the living room and wiping her fat red hands on her blue-checked gingham apron. "You don't say! What is it?"

"This abominable literature! Oh Em, we're ruined! Charlotte is under the sway of those terrible Madisons far more than we ever realized!"

"I told you so, didn't I!" added Aunt Em dryly, looking archly at Cora.

189

"Yes, you did but I thought it couldn't be so bad as this. Why Em, this letter sounds like they were engaged. I had no idea things had gone as far as all that!"

"You had no idea?" stated Em, "Cora Pendelton, don't tell me you're that blind. Why the night of that party over there, I could tell it by their actions, plain as day. Ain't you never learned yet that love thrives on opposition and laughs at locksmiths?"

"Here come Pa and Charlotte now," announced Jane boldly. "I'd be ashamed if I were she!"

Tom Pendelton and Charlotte, returning from the scene of the Manning's suicide, entered the house rather quietly and began to look for the other members of the family. Tom pushed open the dining room door, exclaiming, "Oh, here they are!" To their amazement, they beheld a storm-tossed family.

"What is the matter now?" demanded Tom, weary-like. These cyclonic demonstrations were so common they failed to ruffle his curiosity more than slightly.

Cora ignored his query, but with her prominent blue eyes ablaze, she said tartly to Charlotte, "A pretty thing you are, young lady!"

"Now ma, hold on there!" Tom raised his hand protectively, "Charlotte hasn't done anything!"

"Don't you tell me to hold on, Tom Pendelton—I won't do it! I won't have a Mormon in my family! Not if I can help it!"

"A Mormon—who?"

"She's been reading their literature, ain't she? Look at this—and this—! Cora arose and defiantly thrust forward the offending Book of Mormon and the much derided pamphlets.

"Well, what uv it?" demanded Tom rather indifferently.

"What of it? Tom Pendelton!" loudly demanded Cora, "Are you crazy?"

"Crazy? No, I ain't, but I think you are! Jes plum crazy! Leastwise yer actin' it!"

"Humph! You are a nice one! Where's your pride? Any man with a proper amount wouldn't talk like that. Here I've been living with you all these years and put up with you in spite of everything—and now you have to act like this! Whatever are you coming to?"

Jane and Aunt Em glanced at one another significantly and then at Charlotte, who stood with her back to the radio, white-faced, head up and silent.

"That's old stuff, Cora," answered Tom evenly, "that don't even faze me anymore. You know perfectly well it isn't true. I've always been good to you. If Charlotte wants to be a Mormon, you nor I ain't got no right to interfere. This is a free country, ain't it? Leastwise I always calculated religious freedom wuz a strong point with them Fourth 'o July speakers."

"I suppose you will say we haven't anything to say if she wants to marry one either. Look at this, will you? Now maybe you will wake up." She handed out Andy's letter.

"If Charlotte wants to marry Andy Madison, she can as far as I'm concerned," Tom's eyes met Cora's blazing ones rather calmly. "He asked me fer her this morning, like a gentleman, and I told him 'Yes'."

"You did!!" screamed Cora, almost beside herself with fury. Jane and Aunt Em were white and still, completely shocked.

"Of course, I did, what's wrong with him? You don't have a word to say about it, neither do I. If they want to git married they will in spite of everything, jes like you and I did!"

Cora, dumbfounded, stood like a rock and glared first at Tom, then at Charlotte.

"Very well then, Tom Pendelton, if that's your stand— now I'll take mine. Take your things, young lady, and leave this house immediately! I claim you no longer – you are no daughter of mine!!!

Charlotte's expression was one of humility and filled Tom with pity! But with gentle pride, she turned and walked across the dining room to the stairs. After she had left, Tom turned and followed her silently up to her room.

Jane was filled with exultation and neither she nor Aunt Em made any move to stop Charlotte. Indifferently, the three women sat in silence. It seemed inevitable that she would go.

The stillness of the room was soon broken, however, by Tom coming down the narrow stairs, three steps at a time. He burst into the room, so thoroughly angry he was red in the face.

"Who the devil tore up Charlotte's room like that? You did it, didn't you, Jane?"

"Yes I did, I had a right."

"No human being has a right to treat another like that! Git right up there and put everything back like you found it!"

"I have no intention of doing such a thing," stated Jane shrugging her shoulders nonchalantly.

"Oh, you have no intention, heh? Well, I have! If I tell you to go, you will!!"

"I'm of age and can do as I please!"

"Not in my house and act like that!! Git!!!"

"I won't," replied Jane defiantly, looking him straight in the eyes and narrowing her eyes hatefully.

"Alright then!"—and without any more concern than lifting a forkful of hay, Tom reached forward and quietly lifted his exasperating daughter onto his angular lap as he dropped into a straight-backed chair. Before she could breathe a syllable of her astonishment, the effects of his broad brown palm were felt in no uncertain manner, exactly where she bent over his knees.

"I don't take talk from no one of this risin' generation like that, do you hear?"

With a vigorous shake that loosened the last fiber of her stubborn will, whether she realized it at the moment or not, Tom set her soundly down.

"Now," he blazed, "not another word out of you. Go up there and clean that room!!"

Jane went.

Stillness reigned a moment in the spacious living room – then Cora said defiantly, "Tom Pendelton! Do you realize just what you've done!!"

"I do, my dear, for once in my life I've made myself master of my own house. Jes' what I should have done thirty years ago!!"

"Now, I'm goin' to take my youngest daughter to town and buy her some decent clothes. There is not a thing in that room up there that hasn't a hole in it all the way from the size of a plate ter a milk bucket. And I'm not bringing her home again, this isn't a fit place for such a fine girl to live even if you still wanted her. When and if you ever see her again, she will be Mrs. Andrew Madison, God bless her!"

Without so much as a backward glance at his wife, Tom suddenly left the room. He went to the garage and took the handsome new sedan, driving it up to the yard gate where he waited until Charlotte came downstairs and climbed in beside him.

Aunt Em began to cry softly into her faded apron as they drove down the lane—but Cora's heavy face was set and hard.

"Of all the abominable men!" she burst out furiously, "he is the worst. Why do people have to go crazy over a fool religion, Em, and tear up every bit of peace and happiness that is left in a home. Goodness knows, those Mormons have a repulsive name enough. I'd rather be content to go on in the same old way as our decent fathers and mothers did, than to make myself and family the laughin' stock."

"Aw, Tom ain't a bad sort, Corie, ye jes think it now, 'cause yer mad at him. Wait 'til yer a widder like me, then ye'll think he wuz pure gold. As fer folks goin' crazy over religion, I don't know why they take such crazy streaks. I'm too old to be a'workin' myself up studyin' all their ideas—so I let them be. I wouldn't feel so bad if I wuz you, you can't order yer children's lives and ye ain't responsible fer her no more, regardless uv what folks may say. As fer Jane, she was always a spunk and Tom made her mind fer once. Thet ain't so bad. Ye know yerself if you hadn't got to marry Tom Pendelton the world would've been all ashes and dust."

Cora never made Em any answer. A strained atmosphere crept into the room. Aunt Em felt it and saw that Cora was in a gulf of self-pity and had better be left alone—so she arose and went to the cellar where she had left the freshly churned butter.

Upstairs, Jane stiffened her already tight lips as she bent here and there straightening up Charlotte's room. Her eyes flashed a fresh fury if that were possible.

"He thinks he can spank me and get away with it, does he? Well, I'll show him something that will make him never try it again. This bit of rising generation don't take things like that! As for Charlotte taking the road she has—I think she's a fool. I won't be bound down by stupid religion. I intend to do as I please and have a few things in life outside of this miserable dump!"

Chapter 12 All Clad in White

Elvira Hudnut was just putting the finishing touches to a handsome vase full of pink and lavender asters on her center table when a knock came on her screen door.

"Well, I'll be blest—if it ain't Charlotte Pendelton and her father! Come right in, it's been a regular coon's age since ye wuz over here."

"Sure has," said Tom rather wistfully, as they came in and sat down.

Elvira looked up keenly at him and read the story of sorrow in his troubled blue eyes.

"I wish ye would come oftener, Tom. People nowadays ain't es sociable es they used to be. All we kin think uv now is gittin somewhere—then gittin back."

"Well, I brought you a visitor fer a few days. I hope it won't be no trouble ter you—I don't know whut else ter do about it."

"You don't say, now thet is jes grand fer me. I get kinda lonesome—like fer young folks. I ain't no girl in looks anymore but, Tom, thet ain't no sign the human heart ever grows old."

"Let her stay then until after the weddin', Elvira?" Tom asked sadly. "Things ain't jes as pleasant at home as they might be. But I always figured every soul has a God-given right ter choose it's religious belief and it's mate fer life. I can't see why Andrew Madison wouldn't make a good husband fer my girl, so I stood up fer her, Elvira."

Elvira's faded blue eyes flashed instant approval to his words and she nodded her head, attentively. Her heart was touched and she pitied this worthy father in his loneliness, for she saw that through the years Cora had suffered herself to become apart in spirit from Tom.

"You are 'zactly right there, Tom," she said soothingly. "I allus knew ye had the best o' sense. Charlotte kin make herself ter home here jes like she wuz my girl as long as she likes. You know, Tom, my baby girl, Lillie, died thirty-three years ago this September—an I ain't never hed the privilege uv havin' girls around."

"Her weddin' clothes en everything from hats to trunks is in the car. Shall I bring them in now? I've got to be movin' along; it will soon be milkin' time."

"Yes, Tom, bring 'em right in, and put 'em in that spare bedroom jes off the sitting room. I ain't hed no company in there fer two years but I keep it ready all the time. Then, Tom, ye better come back tonight to the baptismal service about half past eight. We are goin' ter drive down by thet giant old sycamore tree close ter Lucy's place and be immersed there. It's about the only fittin' spot along the high banks of the river. After the service we'll all come home to the little supper I've got ready en enjoy ourselves. The elders will not be here after ter'morrie."

"Thank you, Elvira, I'll come," answered Tom graciously. Then he went to the car and brought Charlotte's things into the bedroom. He kissed his daughter tenderly and, thanking Elvira for her kindness, he departed.

Elvira's house was very quaint to Charlotte. There was nothing modern about it. It seemed to her that she had stepped into another world; the peace and calm which brooded everywhere over the spacious old two-storied red brick house was full of revelation of the ways of other days. From its white carved trim under the wide spreading eaves to the elegant lace woodwork which ran from one tall slender white porch post to another, it spoke of a day that had closed before she had ever opened her eyes. There was a gracious genteel quality hovering about the old place which gave it an atmosphere of exquisite hospitality into which the present culture and breeding would hardly fit with ease.

The inside of the home was just as fascinating. The ample sized rooms were graced with very high ceilings and the walls papered in delicate gold-traced flowers on a cream background or else paneled with a narrow gilt molding. The green and brown flowered carpets ran clear to the walls on whose satin sheen surface rested the fastidious lace curtains of olden days, spread out like a fan to reveal the elegantly plumed birds-of-paradise intricately woven in them. These were surrounded by the most astonishing drapes of forest-green satin, edged with pearl-ball fringe, that Charlotte had ever seen. They fell to the floor in a long shimmering sweep where they lay in soft crumples and folds. Richly carved gilt-framed mirrors reflected the enchantment of the rooms, which were graced by quaintly carved and polished walnut furniture, upholstered in flowered plush and white leather. A marvelous white polar-bearskin rug lay smoothly in front of a slender legged davenport and the decorative feature of the many silk-shaded lamps, that sat here and there among the bric-a-brac, was their gleaming crystal drop-fringe.

Here and there on the graceful tables stood delicate creations of various hues of artificial flowers under round glass domes. These were so quant and prim. So unreal by comparison with the flowers of this day and age that they made Charlotte smile. She could easily imagine the elegantly dressed ladies and precise gentlemen who would perfectly complement such a house. She laughed softly to herself at the idea of the ladies fainting nowadays and calling for the smelling salts, then being presented with adorable little French bouquets which expressed a solicitation for their welfare.

"How do you like this old place, honey?" queried Elvira tenderly with her eyes a twinkle.

"It is quite beautiful to me, Aunt Elvira," Charlotte replied candidly.

"I keep it jes like it is—to fit my old time ways. I ain't much on changin' things. This is the way we lived when I wuz young."

"I wouldn't change a thing here—these pictures of roses, lilacs, and violets—Aunt Elvira, why don't we have things like that anymore. I like the white frames with gilt trimmings."

"Oh shaw, child, people have grown sophisticated an they jes think anything like thet is too simple for words. I allus allowed it wuz the most marvelous miracle, how the great Creator could bring flowers en leaves out uv an insignificant wooden stem. I love to see 'em in the winter, hangin' there, it sorta cheers me up."

"I love the white bear rug, too, Aunt Elvira, it is very handsome."

"Oh thet, my husband brought it to me frum Alaska, when he come back ter marry me—I've kept it years en years now, but law, it ought ter wear well, there ain't no little ones around."

"I believe the elders are coming, Aunt Elvira, they look so awfully tired. See?"

"Yes, that's them alright. This is terrible hot weather, and they ain't used to our climate—leastwise, they say they always have cool nights in the mountain country."

"Oh, here is Miss Charlotte!"   exclaimed Elder Thorensen as he came in with Elder Barton. He shook hands with her heartily and at the same time proceeded to pull out his white handkerchief and mop his forehead.

"Sit down, folks, and rest a bit," invited Elvira graciously. "It's tolerable cool in here, but perhaps not as cool as 'em mountain valleys you been dreamin' about, Elder Thorensen."

"Aunt Elvira says you are going away tomorrow, Elder Thorensen," said Charlotte.

"Yes, we have to go back to Chicago—where we will be released. I'm going home to work in the Logan Temple and Elder Barton here is going back to get married there."   Thorensen's eyes sparkled with a humorous twinkle and he threw a teasing look at Barton, who being a very shy young man colored highly under the banter.

After a light supper, Charlotte and Elvira went to prepare themselves for the service. When they came into the sitting room again, they found the Madisons, Dr. Stone and Tom Pendelton had arrived. The elders came in with George and Charlie, all clad in white.

There was a solemnity about the little gathering that breathed a touch of awe. Elvira's angular form, clothed in her high-necked and long-sleeved white dress seemed strangely softened, while Charlotte appeared a luscious white rose in Andy's admiring eyes.

"Now friends, if we are all ready," said Elder Thorensen as he arose, "we will attend to this service. But before we do, let us have prayer and ask Heavenly Father to bless this evening's work for great power and good in this life."

Accordingly they all knelt in a circle. Dr. Stone found himself beside Becky who seemed entirely absorbed in the moment's devotion. He felt a great desire to join heart and soul in the spirit of the occasion; but doubts—shadowy yet stronger than steel bands—prevented his doing so. It seemed to him that his prayer could not even penetrate the ceiling—let alone ascend to a throne of grace.

On the other side of the room knelt Lucy. Lucy, of the humble ways and retiring spirit. Her eyes filled with a tender mist and lest the happy tears overflow and trace her cheeks, she gently wiped them away on her delicate lace handkerchief. Her heart was as usual rather numb, too full for words—all she could murmur was "Praise thy holy name, Father, for bringing this work to pass!"

The fervent prayer of thanksgiving and blessing over, the little company departed in their cars to the foot of the giant sycamore that stood so like a sentinel on the bank of the placid Wabash near Becky's home.

There, filled by the Spirit of the Lord, Elder Thorensen immersed each one and raised them unto the new life in Christ Jesus. It seemed to Tom Pendelton, as Charlotte was laid under the water, that every tie that bound her to him, in the old life they had always known, was broken. Strong man that he was, his heart quivered in a spasm of sorrow, for he had not the witness of the Holy Spirit to comfort him—hence he suffered as one bereaved.

The four new members of the Church repaired to private quarters that had been arranged for their convenience, and changed their wet clothes. After which, they were confirmed by both of the elders.

Dr. Stone thought he had never witnessed so simple a rite and the thought persistently crept into his mind—was it of any use after all. Away down deep he was troubled again as he had been when he read Thorensen's gift book. The foundations of his disbelief were shaken and left trembling. He felt it must be true—but it was a mighty struggle to even admit the thought. It was no sooner done than the gossamer clouds of doubt again swept through his mind and he felt the power of delusion, which obscured the glory of what he would have liked to believe. In perplexity, he picked up his hat and joined the little company as they got into their cars to return to Elvira's.

As he did so, his troubled eyes met Becky's serene blue ones for a long instant. He felt drawn to her and would have liked to take her in his arms had they been alone. But he realized a vast expanse lay between them. How could he ever ask this slip of a girl, so sublime in her simple faith, to join her life with that of an unbeliever? He felt that such a marriage would be nothing but a solemn mockery for her, in which her spiritual aspirations would be permanently blighted, inch by inch. Rather than drag her down to his level, he would remain silent, until perhaps some day the right moment would come to speak.

Becky saw his attitude in a dazed way. She had repeatedly prayed the Lord send an understanding spirit between them. Looking into the depths of his eyes for that one instant tore away the veil which had kept her mind in wondering obscurity as to his station along the road of life. She saw with supreme joy that he stood directly under the sign of the crossroads and that a terrific struggle against tradition, evil reports, and a desire to believe the simple old time gospel was waging in his soul. She knew now that the battle was half won— because the foundations were shaken and she prayed fervently in her heart for the blessed Christ to give him a real testimony of the divinity of His great work.

Elvira and Lucy saw the two standing there and recognized the struggle as well. They then exchanged a quiet look, their faces reflecting mutual understanding.

Lucy sadly shook her head while Elvira's thoughts ran to the days when she too was young.

"All lovers think," meditated Lucy, "that no one sees and knows their little love tale; but how plain it is for all the world to read. God bless those two children and untangle the difficulty he is in."

In the quiet dusk they rode home. Becky let her hand lay imprisoned in the doctor's strong one, out of sight of the inquisitive eyes. It was the first time it had been like this between them and a bond was woven that was stronger than death, beyond the power of man to describe. It filled both with humility and the exalted spirit of sacrifice. They witnessed the experience of the ennobling quality of true love and were pledged one to the other without the need of mortal speech.

Before long the little group arrived again at Elvira's house, where in the elegance of the old-time rooms they sat and chatted happily while their hostess saw that a summertime treat of ice cream and angel food cake was served to each guest, using her dearly cherished Haviland china plates.

"Elder Barton, get out thet flute uv yours—this is a time fer rejoicin'," said Elvira after all the refreshments were finished.

"I will if Thorensen will sing."

Elder Thorensen, very much at home and supremely happy, gladly sang some quaint old tunes that the pioneers sang as they crossed the plains with their handcarts and ox teams.

When he had finished, the charm of the evening was complete; the party fell into groups of twos and threes and wandered onto the porch or settled back in their restful chairs. Time slipped away in pleasant wishes for the safe journey of the elders on the morrow and the expression of the delight they had had as they worked among them.

As the little company began to break up, Andy spoke to his mother in a whisper. With a little flutter of joy that sent the blood in waves of pink over her white cheeks, Lucy turned and addressed her friends.

"My dears," she stated happily, "I am pleased to announce that my son, Andrew will be married to Miss Charlotte Pendelton tomorrow afternoon in Riverdale at the County Clerk's office—after which, when we go West and can get our temple recommends, they will be sealed for eternity in the Salt Lake Temple."

Exclamations of joy and happiness flooded the room.

Dr. Stone grasped Andy's hand. "I wish you every joy, old fellow," he said tensely. "After the ceremony I will be on my way, perhaps we shall meet again soon."

"Land sakes!" gasped Elvira, "this has turned out to be a momentous evening. I don't know whut 'zactly to call hit—I reckon it's a combination party!"

"Yes," said George dryly, "there ain't no end to the surprises in this life; I don't suppose it would be out uv place, since Charlie is agoin' ter marry Ellen Thatcher.

You might as well be lookin' fer my announcement too—if I kin find me a right smart girl."

"You are going to Utah, young man, do you hear!" exclaimed Elder Thorensen cheerfully. "The pretty girls are not rare out there, nor the smart ones either—so a hint to the wise is sufficient."

"Yeah, men are jes like sheep," put in Tom knowingly, "when one gets the idea of weddin', faith 'en they all go over the fence pell-mell."

Amid much rejoicing and the saying of farewells, Andy approached Charlie and they agreed to settle the legal matters pertaining to the purchase of the Madison farm the following morning.

"We had better get things straightened out, for the Madisons will all be on their way to Utah inside of a month," stated Andy.

As Becky came out of the house after telling Charlotte goodbye, she passed Dr. Stone talking to Elvira. They seemed much taken with their subject and as the doctor warmly shook his hostess's hand, he exclaimed,

"It is agreed then!" To which Elvira spoke approvingly and added delightedly,

"I'm so glad you asked me!"

Becky wondered what it was they were talking about but let it pass from her mind as it didn't concern her.

The doctor joined her on the way to the car. There was a strange something that was a bit baffling between them. They wished, yet they dared not wish too deeply. Looking tenderly into Becky's eyes, Dr. Stone whispered,

"I must go away, Becky darling, pray that I may return."

Before she could reply, her mother and Andy joined them and the homeward journey was begun.

As Tom Pendelton was driving home along his lonely stretch of river road, he thought he passed Jane in Cecil Manning's flashy roadster, going toward Riversdale.

"It's a great time to be going somewhere," he said tersely.

When he came into the house he found Cora very much awake, enthralled in the vulgar trash of the latest "True Story" magazine.

"Where is Jane?" Tom demanded.

"Upstairs in bed," Cora answered sourly.

"I saw her just now, I think, in young Manning's car. What do you mean by letting her go off at this time of night—it's time to be coming, not going?"

"If you don't believe what I say—come on, Tom Pendelton, and I'll show you!" Cora threw down her magazine in fierce ill humor and proceeded up the stairs, followed by her irate husband.

They found Jane's room empty. Empty as a prison cell. No girl — no clothes — nothing but a note pinned to a pillow, in which she said she and Cecil were going to try marriage in companionate style and if they found it worked, they would get properly tied up afterwards.

"Hell," exploded Tom and his face turned ashen white.

"They will eventually marry, Tom, why get so angry? That's the modern trend; people have sense nowadays!"

"Marry!" sneered Tom infinitely disgusted. "Marry! Why woman, that stuff is older than Sodom en Gomorrah!"

With a bitter laugh, he turned and left Cora standing in Jane's room. He stumbled down the stairs into the night again. Alas, poor Tom was like a stricken animal. He was mute before his God; but that did not keep his work-worn hands from clutching his thin gray hair in despair or his crushed heart from beating on and on in agony.

Chapter 13 Mountain Country, Utah

It was some fourteen months later in a western city, nestled close to the everlasting hills, near the giant American Dead Sea, that a throng of people were gathering in a great tabernacle, situated near a mighty temple built of beautiful gray stone unto the ancient Jehovah.

Three travelers, who had but several hours earlier arrived in the city and put up at the most comfortable hotel near the famous square, were mingled with the crowd and presently found seats in the back of the horse-shoe balcony.

It was a glorious bright October Sabbath Day and a general conference of the Latter-Day Saints was in session. The sweet-toned organ burst forth under the skilled fingers of the impassioned organist in tones of rejoicing and glory to the King of Kings. Everywhere, Saints could be seen grasping the hands of this old friend or that, rejoicing in the privilege of once again attending the conference.

The newcomers partook of the spirit of the occasion and felt that they had come home, after much weary wandering, to their own kin.

At length President Grant arose and in his fine commanding voice announced that they would sing, "Come, Come ye Saints."

"I think most everyone knows this song." he said, "but for the benefit of all those who are strangers among us, we will sing this famous old Mormon hymn."

From the first powerful sweeping chords of the prelude, the congregation felt a welding together of spirit, that caused the soul to soar on mighty wings of praise. The congregation together with the choir and leaders of the church sang as one voice–

Come, come ye saints, no toil nor labor fear,
But with joy wend your way.
Though hard to you this journey may appear,
Grace shall be as your day.
'Tis better far for us to strive,
Our useless cares from us to drive,
Do this and joy your hearts will swell,
All is well! All is well!

The great company of saints sang magnificently the three remaining verses, also in a manner which stamped the song as a masterpiece of thanksgiving, praise, faith and hope. Its sublime words called forth all the courage in a human heart and bade the soul no longer languish but become the conqueror of every temporal ill.

The congregation seated themselves and an elder came forward who offered a prayer of thanks for the day and the choice blessings the giver of all good gifts had so graciously bestowed upon the nation. After which the organ began to play a tender prelude and a dark-haired young singer arose from the famous choir and came and stood by the organ in plain view of the audience.

"The Lord is my shepherd, I shall not want,
He maketh me to lie down in green pastures,
He leadeth me beside the still waters,
He restoreth my soul."

Through the rest of the twenty-third psalm, the thrilling young voice wended its way with ease and joyous expression. Like a harpist plucking the strings of his glorious instrument, the singer stirred the chords of each soul present and caused it too, to rejoice with her in the glories of her God. Clearly she was inspired and gifted with her rare gift for that express purpose; and she used it with a freedom and spirit that was amazing.

"It is she, it's Becky," softly whispered one of the travelers to himself. "There is not another like her in this world to me!"

"Didn't I tell ye," answered the old lady joyfully, "thet she had it in her to be jes like thet. God bless her—jes listen. Ain't thet grand?"

The song ended in a glorious cadenza and the singer took her seat in the large choir. President Grant next announced that the speaker would be Elder Talmadge. He preached a lengthy sermon on the fruitless reasoning of atheistic philosophy, with an intelligence and power that left his hearers convinced that he spoke as one indeed who had authority.

The old lady turned to a strange gentleman who sat beside her and said,

"Thet Dr. Talmadge is a real apostle, ain't he? I niver heared much uv him before, but I must say he's a preacher uv the gospel after me own heart. He talks jes like Peter er Paul must have done. This is a good place ter be. I never ran across a city with a spirit in it jes like this one be. We noticed it when we first came."

"No ma'm," answered the gentleman graciously with a smile. "I don't expect you ever did. This is the city where the Temple of the Lord is built and His peace is over it, if you are in tune and can feel it. Dr. Talmadge is one of our dearly beloved leaders and bears a powerful testimony, ma'm. He is mighty in declaring the truth of the Restored Gospel."

The congregation sang again and after several other short speakers, the closing song was sung and the organ swelled forth in a grand recessional that seemed so wonderfully inspired, the old lady would not have been at all surprised had she seen angels of the Lord in the midst of the congregation or hovering over it.

The immense crowd was soon out of the tabernacle and the three strangers found themselves waiting patiently for the appearance of the young singer, who had lingered talking to the organist. At length she approached them accompanied by an elderly woman, evidently her mother.

"Lucy Madison!" cried the strange old lady, hurrying forward. "Ye ain't changed a bit."

To Lucy's astonishment she suddenly found herself in a pair of wrinkled old arms that were strangely familiar, and looking into a pair of faded blue eyes that still knew how to twinkle.

"Elvira Hudnut, you old rogue! Where on earth have you been?"

"Been?" laughed Elvira contagiously, "why we've been all over, ain't we, George?"

"We certainly have," answered that deep-toned Indianian. "We saw everything, I reckon."

Dr. Stone did not answer anything, he was literally carried away by the sight of the modest gray-clad figure which stood demurely by Lucy's side.

"Where did you go," quizzed Lucy, surprised. "I kept looking and looking for letters that never came and we kept wondering and wondering why you didn't write 'till we nearly worried ourselves sick. Until at last we thought maybe you considered you had better drop us entirely."

"Well, Lucy, I calculate it wuz no way to treat you and you may think it wuz some wild goose chase we tuck, but we've even been ter the land o' Egypt—and that's only one o' the places."

"Tut, tut, I ain't old—leastwise I ain't felt it yit. If ye could jes hev seen me crawlin' thru thet old pyramid in them new fangled hikin' clothes o'mine, sometimes pretty near on my tummy, you'd a'thought I wuz kin ter spring chickens, wouldn't she hev, George?"

"Law yes! I never did see sech a woman. She insisted on ridin' the camels out to the place en nothin' would do but thet she go clear to the top uv it—let alone scramble all thru it too."

"Land sakes," laughed Elvira merrily, "I wouldn't a'missed it fer the world. Jes think, Lucy, I went plum thru it—clear down ter the 'bottomless pit'! Did ye jes ever fancy me getting' in sech a place, en comin' back?"

Lucy squeezed her old friend's hand joyfully and remarked, "I'll never rest until I immediately hear the rest of this thrilling tale. Come on home with us, all of you, and tell us what you've been up to. Our car is parked over on the west side—Andy, Charlotte, and the baby are waiting in it."

"The baby," gasped Elvira, "Lucy Madison, air ye a grandma?"

"I am!" stated Lucy proudly. "I have a grandson, Andrew Jr., one month old."

"Well, I'll be blest, but thet is sure somethin' nice to hear. Let's go see thet baby right now."

The little group of happy folk started toward the car. Andy saw them coming and jumped out of the car to meet them.

"Upon my word," he exclaimed excitedly, "If I ain't found my old sweetheart again." He soundly kissed her.

"An I hear ye air a fond Daddy!" cried Elvira happily greeting Charlotte and peering at the tiny pink baby while Andy greeted George and Dr. Stone.

"Humph! He ain't a bit like his ma," commented Elvira, "thet will never go fer a boy. Jes look at them long fingers o' his'n. He's like his pa—he'll be a real fiddler frum the looks o' things."

Everyone laughed while Andy said, "Let us hope, Aunt Elvira, that he does become a great Mormon violinist."

"The folks are going home with us, Andy," said Lucy, "let's be going. We have a great deal to talk over." Lucy and Elvira seated themselves followed by George, Becky, and Dr. Stone.

Soon they were purring along in the big car, heading north of the city to a little town called Bountiful. Here Andy turned from the paved highway into the modest driveway of a well-kept place, built back from the busy thoroughfare a good distance, and situated in a fine grove of cottonwood trees.

"Welcome home, folks!" cried Andy as he jumped out and threw open the car doors. "Welcome to our Utah home, the best and dearest of all."

221

The happy hours which followed were spent in exploring the charming gray-stone house and the twenty-acre farm surrounding it.

Lucy said, after Elvira had admired the house so immensely, "It is something like our old house, Elvira, in that it too is early American. I thought too much change of atmosphere would make us all homesick. It is modern too, you see, and that is better than the old place where we had to wash with a gasoline engine. But I didn't let them build a second story, I got tired of going up and down stairs to clean back there—I thought this would be easier. Sometimes I sit in this grove of trees in my easy chair and pretend I'm back home a few seconds. But now that you have seen the place and I've told you most everything, Elvira, let's sit down, I want to hear the rest of that account of yourself—and from the beginning."

"There ain't much ter tell," replied Elvira meekly, "'cept thet Dr. Stone tuck the notion thet maybe George and me would like ter go over ter the Holy Land and Egypt and all 'em places to look around fer a spell. I guess he figured since he was practically an infidel or whatever you call it, that he'd have to start frum the ground up, if he was iver goin' to straighten out his dilemma and make himself worthy of Becky.

"Anyhow," continued Elvira, "we allowed an how we'd really like ter do it. Jest to be seeing the sights mostly, but I sort o' had a notion it wouldn't do no harm if I traipsed along to put a little plain common sense into his head if he got too involved and befuddled in all his studying. I figure I ain't too old ter know true love when I see hit, and I wanted to make sure he came back to Becky. He's too good a man to lose, I figured. I knew it'd be hard for him en sometimes I think he jes about gave it all up; but finally he jes had to admit thet Jesus was the Christ and our Lord and Savior. Then o'course there was all the business of finding the right Christian church. He couldn't take anybody else's word fer it, he had to study and compare them all himself. George en me did try to not influence him too much but it was this question uv authority thet finally got him."

"Yes, that's the final decision always, Elvira, then everything else unfolds so simply. And what did you do all this time and where all did you go?"

"Well, Lucy, we went first to England o'course, and me en George got busy on thet genealogy uv ours and traced it clear back ter the Norman Conquest en past on several uv our lines. George turned out to be a right smart genealogist once he got started. I allowed I wuzn't very proud to be hitched up with a line of Merovingian kings, they bein' so disgraceful en coarse actin' en all—but

George said it didn't make no difference, they were jes as much a child uv the Almighty as I be.

"Then part uv the time that we stayed in London, I went ter all the museums and old churches, Lucy—pokin' in en around them musty old ancient buildings till I actually got ter doin' hit in my sleep en nearly walked into a strange bedroom one night in the little hotel where we stayed. George, he was so scandalized, he said he wouldn't be responsible fer no woman he had to tie ter her bedpost 'fore he went to his room—so he up and tuck me to France. It weren't much better there, as there's jes as many old cathedrals en historic buildings there es in England. Italy too, fer thet matter. Anyhow George en the Doc were jes crazy ter see Palestine so we packed up again. It sure did my heart good to know that Orson Hyde had dedicated thet land to the 'return o' the Jews'—it has suffered so long. Makes a person realize how small and insignificant their troubles are, to stand on they land where Jesus walked."

"And did you really see the pyramids?" urged Lucy.

"You bet your boots, we did. We went out there after we'd seen all those dried up mummies in the museums at Cairo and King Tut en all his possessions too. I sure wish you'd been along—we did hev a wonderful time."

"Well, I'm delighted to think you went, Elvira, it really must have been an exciting trip."

"I knew you'd think so, Lucy. What have ye been doing since ye got settled?"

"I've been working in the Temple, Elvira, and oh my dear, it is the most joyous thrill of a lifetime. We all had to wait one year before we could get our recommends then the children got married for eternity and I was sealed to my Robert and our children sealed to us. Since then I've been doing a great deal, with the children's help, on our genealogy too. Father's and Mother's work is done and they are sealed also—oh Elvira, it is a blessed work. I never was so happy in my whole life."

"I wish I could find a farm around here close, so I could go in with you too. We've got so much work to do," wished Elvira wistfully.

"Farms are hard to find, Elvira, we had a time to find this one, but we'll look around, don't worry."

"Mother! Aunt Elvira!" called Becky from the front door of the little cottage. "Come into the house, we are going to have a real watermelon party, and there are muskmelons too."

The dear old friends arose from their easy wicker chairs and went into the house—where they found Dr. Stone standing in the dining room door with a big white apron tied around him. He was smiling broadly, showing all his handsome white teeth in a boyish grin.

"Ain't Utah grand?" he teased.

"It is fer a fact," declared Elvira warmly as she spied the delicious slices of melon which graced each blue-willow plate. "I'm jes tickled pink ter think I cum!"

"Say, Mother," said George eagerly, "Andy says there is a fine little fruit farm west of here fer sale. How would ye like ter live among apricot, peach, and cherry trees fer the rest of yer days?"

"Oh fiddle sticks, ye don't mean thet heaven es come down this early, do ye? Will ye plant some uv these melons betwixt the trees fer me?" Elvira asked wistfully.

"Sure, en they say there is a real red brick house on the place with white woodwork lace trim."

"Aw get out," exclaimed Elvira a bit surprised. "If ye don't stop tellin' sich things, George Hudnut, I'll begin ter believe there never wuz a thing ter all this sacrificin' story we saints hear about, but thet everything is restored ter us in Zion en more too."

"Oh, but that is true, Auntie darling," approved Charlotte, "we never give up anything but we find it's compensations here. Even my father and Leander are being restored to me."

"How does it come?" asked Elvira in amazement, between bites of melon.

"Mother died, you know, five months ago from a heart attack and Aunt Em went to live with her daughter in Elkhart. So that left Papa and Leander alone. I wrote to them about what a wonderful place this was —so much fruit and everything. Papa wrote back that he was selling out and I look for them any day now—that was a month ago."

"If thet is the way things is aworkin' out, honey, I calculate George en me hed better begin to look after thet there place he wuz tellin' about. Charlie en Ellen will be makin' me a visit too. Anyhow I'm gettin' plum tired o' trottin' around. I want ter curl up on my old sofie, with the white bear rug spread out at my feet, look again at my geraniums abloomin' in my winder, en go ter sleep. I guess I'm kinda homesick after so much gallivantin'."

Chapter 14 Will You Sing For Me

The mountains were no longer bathed in the soft rose afterglow of the setting sun, when a few hours after Lucy's guests had departed to the city, Dr. Stone returned to the little stone house built back from the road.

The yellow leaves that fluttered on the great cottonwood trees, so mildly in the mild October breeze, were gently loosening their hold and sailing artfully one by one to sleep, upon the well-kept lawn. Becky waited by a giant bed of verbenas, bordering the front of the gray and white stone cottage. Dr. Stone was entranced by the sight of the girl he loved. In her pink flowered organdie dress, with its simple round neck, dainty puff sleeves, and a graceful skirt, ruffled from her slender ribbon-caressed waist to the hem, she was all he had ever dreamed of.

The look of adoration in his dark eyes, as he came eagerly toward her, made Becky feel rather shy and she would gladly have fled. But as she looked into his face, he saw that she was happy. Her complexion gleamed a soft pink and her cornflower-blue eyes were gently alluring. Now she no longer needed to lower her head, letting her black curls fall, and wonder through long, weary hours what had become of her lover. It seemed Paradise that he was in her range of vision again.

"Mother and the folks have gone to Sacrament Meeting," she said.

"Let's sit on the lawn then, until they come."

"Or maybe you'd like to see the new music books I bought the other day in Salt Lake? I'm proud of them— I've wanted something like that for so long."

So together they entered the little front hall and turned into the living room where the beautiful grand piano stood. Becky had brought it with her from Indiana.

"After I see the books, will you sing for me?" he asked gently. "Oh Becky, I do love your singing."

"I do sing better than I did," she replied modestly. "I have been studying at a fine conservatory in the city ever since we came here—both piano and voice. I am wrapped up in the work and would like to improve my voice, if it is good enough, until I am worthy to stand among the best singers. I want to show the world that Latter-Day Saints are not the uncouth people that we are often made out to be."

They sat down on the low chintz-covered davenport at the end of the room and began to look at the handsomely bound music books that she held in her arms.

A series of lead paned French windows, draped in simple ecru silk were open at their left. In front of them stood a mahogany gate-leg table. A scarlet geranium in an antique pot bloomed luxuriantly from its midst. The touch of brilliant flowers added the proper note of life and fascination to the room.

"What do you want me to sing?" she asked as he finished looking at the classical music. "Annie Laurie?"

"By all means, then 'Comin' thru the Rye'."

Becky arose and crossed the room while he came to stand near the curve of the piano. She lit two tall wax candles on either side of her music book and smiled up at him as she seated herself on the piano bench.

Then she began to play, her gentle touch caressing the melody as she went, and her voice leading out as softly as the west wind sometimes blows. It seemed to Dr. Stone that here was the original Annie Lourie herself; he had no need for the Scotch lassie when his heart was so full of this American one. When she had finished, a mist which he quickly tried to hide had gathered in his eyes. He was unable to speak and stood with down-cast eyes looking into the brilliant petals of the scarlet geraniums which stood in the center of the piano on an embroidered shawl.

With a fairy lilt in her voice, the come-hither words of "Comin' thru the Rye" came on to the air. Dr. Stone could not resist a roguish smile nor the twinkle from creeping into his eyes.

"Gosh, Becky," he sighed tenderly, "when you sing like that—"

She smiled delightedly but quickly added graciously—to hide her confusion, "Tell me of your trip to England."

"I'd far rather tell you why I came home." He slid down beside her on the piano bench and the expression on his face made Becky tremble.

"You were gone so long," she murmured with downcast eyes.

"I would never have gone away at all, sweetheart, but I realized I couldn't risk asking you to marry me, unless I was a Mormon also. Becky, my darling, I do love you so. Will you marry me?"

"If you know for sure that the Gospel is true—yes, I'll marry you, Douglas, I've loved you for so long."

"Sweetheart!" he whispered against her hair as he folded her into his strong arms, and found her sweet warm lips with his own in a kiss full of solemn promise and exquisite happiness.

To Becky, this was the moment she had prayed for so earnestly; waiting, day after day, wondering and worrying night after night. Perhaps it was a dream to feel those arms holding her so tenderly, a trick of fancy to find just the right niche on that broad shoulder for her head.

But his low mellow voice reassured her this was no dream, with its promise, "I'll do everything in my power to make you happy, my dearest—I swear I will. I'm the happiest man in the world," and smiling together at the age-old declaration, the lovers unconsciously fell into making plans—plans that from this hour forward would include both of them as one flesh.

"Will you take me to see some of these places you've been, dear? It would be such a lovely honeymoon," whispered Becky against his shoulder. "Wouldn't it be wonderful to see the Sacred Grove and other Church history sites back East?"

"Yes, darling, there is yet a good deal I'd like to see myself, and most important of all, I'm seriously considering the possibility of proving that the Book of Mormon is authentic from the worldly point of view.

From what I've read so far of the histories of the earliest known Indian tribes in Mexico and South America, I'm convinced it can be proved in a scientific way also. We'll take a long trip through those parts of the Country to verify the facts I've already accumulated, make it a glorious honeymoon at the same time, come home and settle down—teaching in one of these western agricultural colleges—and spend our days together in spreading this new and everlasting Gospel."

"My darling," she sighed, "how thankful I am the Lord brought you to me that morning back home in Indiana."

Then as lovers always do, they began to reminisce of the fateful day they met, marveling at the simple and ordinary way such a miraculous event should come about—as though it was all meant to be.

"Just think what an unhappy life I might have lived, an atheist and without you, if I hadn't taken a notion to drop in on my old pal, Andy Madison."

"Yes, you knocking on our screen door was the beginning of a great many things."

"Indeed, it was—your hair was very charming and your lips very red. I adored the blue-checkered dress with such a daring red bow, but it was the dangling apple peeling that did the trick I think."

"I was afraid that had given me away—I was quite aware of the very handsome stranger, darling. I kept telling myself you'd never look at me twice and then there was our difference of religion—how all my dreams have come true. Ours will be a real marriage, Douglas."

"We shall be one, sweet," he tenderly answered, "one in heart, one in mind, one in spirit, living unto the Lord."

"Then dearest, you shall become a king and ruler in the Kingdom of the Lord, forever and ever."

"And you, precious, shall be my queen and priestess, world's without end, through which our love shall develop into glorious fruitfulness—joys that we, as mortals now, cannot even comprehend."

Eight months later on a brilliant day in the first week of May, when the young leaves were shining their brightest on the stately trees and hyacinths and jonquils were standing in their graceful beds under an enlivening morning sun, a beautiful young bride emerged with her gallant husband at her side, from the sacred walls of

God's Holy Temple. She was accompanied by her mother, brother and sister, and Indiana friends.

"God bless you, my children, and prosper you through all eternity," said Lucy, kissing her daughter and wiping her eyes free from tears.

"I'll be blest, Lucy Madison, this is a grand day. Do for goodness sake, stop crying. Ain't we jes goin' ter have the time of our young lives workin' in this here Temple. Shame on ye! Didn't ye git married yerself? Weren't ye as happy as a jenny wren in a blackberry thicket?"

"I was, Elvira! I was," agreed Lucy, blinking back the last of the tears.

"Sure and ye wuz, en if yer old father wuz here this minute, he'd be tellin' ye ter cheer up becuz uv the glories ter cum. Wouldn't he?"

"Perhaps he has been with us for all we know, Elvira," said Lucy, while Douglas laughed merrily at her from beside his exquisite bride.

"Let's not be thinkin' sech things," exclaimed Elvira. "There is a little superstition mixed up with me yet, they the waters uv baptism didn't wash away, I'm afraid. Rather let's be goin' ter thet grand weddin' breakfast ye promised I could give ye, Mrs. Stone."

Becky blushed happily and glanced shyly at Douglas.

"Do ye think ye kin eat today, Becky?" teased George gaily.

"If she don't," said Elvira positively, "It ain't agoin' to be my fault. I ain't calculatin' on letting her starve thru the first meal in her grand new home, ner sendin' her off on her honeymoon on an empty tummy. No siree, not after whut I went thru. They told me ter carry chocolate bars with me when I climbed ter the top uv the pyramid—but I'm here ter tell ye, I'd abetter took ham en eggs."

About The Author

Mary Elizabeth (Taylor) Knickerbocker 1895-1934. The only daughter of a minister, she grew up with two older brothers. She later became a mother to nine children, Gilberta Louise, Harry Gould, John Robert (who lived only five months), Rebecca Ann (who lived only 17 hours), Mary Ellen, and Beverly Jane. The heartbreaking loss of these babies led her to question the comfort and solace offered by the faith in which she had been raised, prompting her to explore other religions more deeply. Upon discovering Mormonism, she found the answers and reassurances she had long sought.

In December of 1927, Luke and Mary brought their family of four children to Ogden, Weber County, Utah and they were baptized into the Mormon Church. Three more children were born to them in Utah: Alfred Luke, William Irvin, and Charlotte Elaine (who lived only one month).

Although Will You Sing For Me is fictional, her character and personality are shining through on every page: the charming girl with sincere thoughtful manners; the talented pianist with beautiful singing voice; the gifted artist depicting beauty, in oils and watercolors, as she had the insight to see it; the lovely sweetheart, happy bride and faithful wife; the tender, loving mother willingly sacrificing herself for her children; the earnest Bible scholar discovering new Truth; the humble poet who stirred emotions with her gift of language; the creative writer who painted beautiful pictures with words; the steadfast convert who loved the Lord, persevered against adversity, and endured to the end.

www.ingramcontent.com/pod-product-compliance
Lightning Source LLC
Chambersburg PA
CBHW060315260626
47160CB00007B/2621